SO MANY BABIES

Four heart-tugging stories about the littlest matchmakers as they find their way through the Buttonwood Baby Clinic and into a family's welcoming arms!

THE BABY LEGACY by Pamela Toth
Special Edition #1299 On sale January 2000

When an anonymous sperm donor tries to withdraw his "contribution," he learns a beautiful woman is eight months pregnant—with *his* child!

WHO'S THAT BABY? by Diana Whitney
Special Edition #1305 On sale February 2000

A handsome Native American lawyer finds a baby on his doorstep—and more than he bargains for with an irresistible pediatrician who has more than medicine on her mind!

MILLIONAIRE'S INSTANT BABY
by Allison Leigh
Special Edition #1312 On sale March 2000

Pretend to be married to a millionaire "husband"? It seemed an easy way for this struggling single mom to earn a trust fund for her newborn. But she never thought she'd fall for her make-believe spouse....

MAKE WAY FOR BABIES! by Laurie Paige
Special Edition #1317 On sale April 2000

All she needed was a helping hand with her infant twins—until her former brother-in-law stepped up to play "daddy"—and walked right into her heart.

Dear Reader,

It's going to be a wonderful year! After all, we're celebrating Silhouette's 20th anniversary of bringing you compelling, emotional, contemporary romances month after month.

January's fabulous lineup starts with beloved author Diana Palmer, who returns to Special Edition with *Matt Caldwell: Texas Tycoon*. In the latest installment of her wildly popular LONG, TALL TEXANS series, temperatures rise and the stakes are high when a rugged tycoon meets his match in an innocent beauty—who is also his feisty employee.

Bestselling author Susan Mallery continues the next round of the series PRESCRIPTION: MARRIAGE with *Their Little Princess*. In this heart-tugging story, baby doctor Kelly Hall gives a suddenly single dad lessons in parenting—and learns all about romance!

Reader favorite Pamela Toth launches Special Edition's newest series, SO MANY BABIES—in which babies and romance abound in the Buttonwood Baby Clinic. In *The Baby Legacy*, a sperm-bank mix-up brings two unlikely parents together temporarily—or perhaps forever....

In Peggy Webb's passionate story, *Summer Hawk*, two Native Americans put aside their differences when they unite to battle a medical crisis and find that love cures all. Rounding off the month is veteran author Pat Warren's poignant, must-read secret baby story, *Daddy by Surprise*, and Jean Brashear's *Lonesome No More*, in which a reclusive hero finds healing for his heart when he offers a single mom and her young son a haven from harm.

I hope you enjoy these six unforgettable romances and help us celebrate Silhouette's 20th anniversary all year long!

Best,

Karen Taylor Richman
Senior Editor

Please address questions and book requests to:
Silhouette Reader Service
U.S.: 3010 Walden Have., P.O. Box 1325, Buffalo, NY 14269
Canadian: P.O. Box 609, Fort Erie, Ont. L2A 5X3

PAMELA TOTH

THE
BABY
LEGACY

Published by Silhouette Books

America's Publisher of Contemporary Romance

Special thanks and acknowledgment
are given to Pamela Toth for her contribution
to the So Many Babies series.

 SILHOUETTE BOOKS

ISBN 0-373-24299-9

THE BABY LEGACY

Visit us at www.romance.net

Printed in U.S.A.

PAMELA TOTH

USA Today bestselling author Pamela Toth was born in Wisconsin, but grew up in Seattle where she attended the University of Washington and majored in art. Now living on the Puget Sound area's east side, she has two daughters, Erika and Melody, and two Siamese cats.

Recently she took a lead from one of her romances and married her high school sweetheart, Frank. They live in a townhouse within walking distance of a bookstore and an ice cream shop, two of life's necessities, with a fabulous view of Mount Rainier. When she's not writing, she enjoys traveling with her husband, reading, playing FreeCell on the computer, doing counted cross-stitch and researching new story ideas. She's been an active member of Romance Writers of America since 1982.

Her books have won several awards and they claim regular spots on the Waldenbooks bestselling romance list. She loves hearing from readers, and can be reached at P.O. Box 5845, Bellevue, WA 98006. For a personal reply, a stamped, self-addressed envelope is appreciated.

IT'S OUR 20th ANNIVERSARY!
We'll be celebrating all year, starting with these fabulous titles, on sale in January 2000.

Chapter One

Mac Duncan stared down at the letter in his hand and swore softly. This was a hell of a way to find out he was going to be a father.

The letter was from the Buttonwood Baby Clinic where he'd left a certain deposit with the fertility department three years before to help out a platonic female friend. Since Linda had changed her mind about having a baby by artificial insemination and was now happily married, Mac had figured it was time for his sperm sample to be destroyed. Spotting the envelope with his incoming mail this afternoon, he'd assumed it contained some kind of consent form for him to sign.

Was he ever wrong.

The brief letter read,

Dear Mr. Duncan,
Our staff is looking forward to helping you and Ms. Megan Malone prepare for the birth of your baby. As per your request, you have both been registered for the next series of childbearing classes at the clinic. Please see the enclosed brochure for details.

Huh?

He hadn't signed up for a childbirth class, he wasn't having a baby—and who the hell was Megan Malone?

Could one of his men be playing a practical joke? No, that didn't make sense. None of them knew about Mac's donation to the clinic.

Slowly he read the letter again, staring hard at the innocent-looking blue script printed on thick, cream paper. Was it possible that some mix-up had occurred and his sperm had actually been used without his permission?

Mac laid the letter on his drafting table, his hands shaking as the implication sank in. This woman, this stranger, could be pregnant with his child.

His stomach did a queasy somersault. And what was this nonsense about a childbirth class? Weren't the names of donors and recipients supposed to be kept confidential? Mac glanced at the enclosed flyer in disbelief. The class was for expectant mothers and their partners, not anonymous donors. Not even if their sperm had been used by accident.

Fury replaced Mac's original confusion. One way or another, a hell of a big mistake had been made and he wanted some answers.

Anger simmering, he grabbed the cordless phone from his desk and punched out the clinic's number from the letterhead. "Dennis Reid," he growled.

Mac and the chief of staff had met at the local health club and sometimes played racquetball. Although Dennis was older than Mac, he was fiercely competitive. If he didn't have answers, he could at least point Mac in the right direction.

Unfortunately Dennis was at a seminar in Denver. "Can I take a message?" the receptionist asked.

"Yes. This is Mac Duncan. There's been a foul-up," Mac said, too impatient to wait. "Let me speak to the person in charge of class registration."

"Just a moment."

Mac sat back, leather chair creaking like an old saddle, and pinched the bridge of his nose.

"I'm sorry," said the same cheerful voice. "She's not available. Perhaps I can help you with that."

"Not unless you're prepared to explain why I'm having a child I knew nothing about and am registered for a class with a pregnant woman I've never heard of." Mac held on to his temper with difficulty, frustration curdling in his gut.

"Just a moment." The annoying cheerfulness was gone from her voice as she put him on hold again. Unable to sit still, he leaped to his feet. His elbow bumped a stack of blueprints and they rolled to the floor. Swearing, he nudged them aside with the toe of his boot. He'd stayed home this morning to get some work done. Too bad the sun and his dog, Rusty, had lured him outside to the mailbox. Now the plans for the Delany project would just have to wait.

After several frustrating minutes, the receptionist came back on the line. "I'm sorry for the delay. I'll access your file now."

There was another pause long enough for Mac to slowly count to ten while he stared out the window overlooking his backyard. The flower beds needed attention, he noticed absently. The warmer weather had brought out the weeds.

"I'm sorry," she said finally. "Patient records aren't coming up on my computer screen. We've been having trouble with the system. Why don't you call back later?"

"Isn't there anyone else who can help me now?" he demanded through gritted teeth.

"Not really, but I can have someone get back to you."

"You do that." He rattled off his number before he hung up. Then he sat back down and reread the letter for the third time. It had to be some kind of clerical error. Any clinic dealing with fertility would take precautions against this kind of breach or they'd be up to their test tubes in lawsuits.

Mac drummed his fingers on his desk. Someone else named Duncan had probably signed up for the class and the letter had been sent to Mac by mistake. It was a computer glitch. No point in getting stressed out.

Not yet, anyway.

He wanted a baby, but not by a stranger. He was thirty-seven and it was past time to start a family, but there was more to fathering a child than just standing at stud like a syndicated racehorse.

He'd been considering the idea of proposing to Justine Connors, the woman he'd been seeing for the past six months, and that was one reason he'd finally gotten around to contacting the clinic about his sperm.

Tying up loose ends was quickly turning into unraveling the Gordian knot.

What if they *had* actually used his sample by mistake? A chill slid down his spine. If not for the letter, he never would have known.

What if a similar notice had been sent to Ms. Malone? She'd certainly know if she was pregnant, and by whom. All he had to do was to ask her.

Mac flipped open the local phone book, found the right page and ran his finger down the column. There was only one M. Malone. She must be single. He reached for the phone and then he hesitated. What was he going to say? Are you having my baby?

Megan Malone hit the Save button on her computer and leaned back in her chair. She'd been working all morning on a vegetarian cookbook and her back was beginning to ache. Megan knew from experience that it was time for a break.

With a self-deprecating grin at her own awkwardness, she heaved herself out of her chair and waddled down the stairs of her townhouse with one hand on the banister and the other cradling her bulging stomach. True to form, her baby had stopped kicking the moment Megan got up.

When she reached the bottom of the staircase, she called to the heap of gray fur dozing in the sun shining through the patio door. The rebirth that spring always brought made it her favorite season.

''Time to get the mail, Cassius.''

The cat, a big gray Persian with gold eyes, didn't even stir. The only indication that he was alive at all was the gentle rise and fall of his stomach.

With a shrug, Megan went outside, breathing in the fresh, sweet air. Sometimes Cassius liked to accompany her, but only if it was his idea. He preferred acting the aristocrat he resembled rather than the bedraggled stray she'd adopted a year ago.

Megan walked out to the cluster of mailboxes in front of her building and retrieved her mail. Turning, she stopped to admire the vivid hues surrounding her—the periwinkle-blue of the sky, the rich green of the velvety lawn, the buttery-yellow daffodils, the waxy white hyacinths and fringe of royal purple crocus that lined the sidewalks.

The complex where she lived was a small one,

two units to a building, all painted cream and trimmed with navy-blue. Megan knew several of her neighbors well enough to exchange a few words, especially since she had started to show. They asked how she felt and when she was due, but so far, at least, no one had mentioned the missing father.

Humming to herself, Megan took her mail inside and sat down at the dining room table to go through it. There was a phone bill, a gourmet cooking magazine, a pre-approved credit card application, a bulky package from one of the publishers for whom she did freelance cookbook indexing, a periodical about cats and a letter from the baby clinic.

She'd called the clinic last week to sign up for the birthing class she'd canceled three months before when her friend Helen, who'd agreed to go with her, had been transferred to Boston. Megan still needed to find a new partner. Since she worked at home and had no family in the area, her options were limited.

In the envelope was a flyer about the class and a letter. As Megan read it, the blood slowly drained from her head, leaving her dizzy.

She'd planned on raising her child alone. Except for the biological father's medical history and a brief physical description, she knew nothing about him. Didn't *want* to know. Deliberately she had picked a donor who wished to remain anonymous, and she'd been assured by the clinic that neither of their identities would ever be revealed to the other.

In the past she had tried to do it the traditional way—meet a man, fall in love, get married and have a family. If Mr. Right was out there, Megan hadn't been able to find him despite several disappointing attempts. The Buttonwood Baby Clinic had offered her an alternative and she'd moved here to take it.

Now she felt betrayed. According to this letter the donor, MacGregor Duncan, was going to be her partner at the new childbirth class.

No, no, no! This was terrible. He never should have been given her name. The people at the clinic were crazy if they thought she'd go along with this arrangement.

Heart racing, Megan grabbed the phone. Not only had she no intention of learning about breathing, contractions and delivery with a perfect stranger, she didn't want some man interfering in her life and the raising of her child. *Her child.* Not his. Not theirs. No shared custody. No meddling. That wasn't the deal.

A few frustrating moments later, Megan replaced the receiver and pressed the heels of her hands to her head. She was too late. Mr. Duncan's notice had been mailed the same day as hers. By now he knew her identity, too. The woman Megan had talked to had been no help at all and Megan had been too upset to insist on speaking with someone else.

She thought about calling them back. Instead she

got up and circled the table, one hand braced on her back. What a mess!

What was she going to do now?

Probably the most sensible plan of action would be to contact the donor herself, but something inside her hated to cross that line. Since she'd become pregnant, she had managed to forget that anyone else had been involved in the process. Now that she knew the donor's name it was more difficult to ignore his existence. Once she spoke to him, heard his voice, it might become downright impossible.

She popped a peanut butter M&M from a bowl on the counter into her mouth. She could just skip the class. No, it was much too late to reschedule. Although she'd spent a considerable part of her childhood taking care of various younger cousins, they hadn't actually been babies. Besides, she knew next to nothing about giving birth.

Perhaps the donor was as surprised by the notice as she was. He must realize that being assigned as her birthing-class partner was an unfortunate clerical error, to quote the girl at the clinic. Unless he assumed it was all Megan's idea. Oh, dear. She had to set him straight and to explain that she wanted nothing to do with him. There was no reason for them to ever meet.

Surely he'd be relieved to know he was off the hook. A man who donated sperm wasn't looking for parental responsibility, child support, weekend visits, diapers, bottles, or anything else that went along with having a baby together—was he?

She had to know his intentions. There was a chance she would need to consult an attorney and find out her rights.

Since when had maternity gotten so complicated?

Before Megan could reach for another M&M, the baby gave her a hard kick. Despite her refusal to be told its gender, she had always thought of it as a boy.

"Hey, champ, how are you doing?" she cooed, rubbing the spot he'd poked. Already she loved this little being, this tiny, precious part of herself. Since she had first decided to become a single parent and raise a child alone, she hadn't had one moment of regret or doubt. Together the two of them would become the family Megan had always longed for.

She picked up the letter again and read the donor's name aloud. "MacGregor Duncan." No question of his ancestry. She didn't care about that—there were probably a few drops of Scottish blood in her own mixed lineage.

The man was a stranger and yet, despite her attempt to ignore his contribution, a part of him was growing inside her. She had been told that he was intelligent, healthy, had medium-brown hair and dark eyes. Before she had known his name, she hadn't given him another thought, but now her curiosity was piqued.

Biting her lip, she shook her head and crumpled up the letter. There were reasons she'd chosen to have this child alone. Best she not forget them.

In the silence of her town home, the sudden shrill

ring of the phone startled both her and Cassius, who raised his head and gave her an accusing glance. Usually Megan let the machine take her calls during her working hours, but this time she picked up the receiver without thinking and said hello.

"Is this Megan Malone?"

At the sound of the deep male voice, a shiver of response slid down her spine. Dratted hormones. "Yes, this is she," she answered warily. Sometimes even telemarketers had attractive voices.

There was another pause, but she could hear breathing. She was about to hang up when a strong suspicion leaped at her. "Mr. Duncan?" she blurted.

"Yes, but how did you know?" He sounded surprised.

"I just read my mail," she said dryly. "When I called the clinic, they told me you'd been sent the same letter I got. I assume you're as stunned as I am by this bizarre turn of events."

"Stunned doesn't begin to describe my reaction," he replied with a thread of humor in his voice that warmed her, despite her wariness. At least the situation hadn't been all his idea.

Megan frowned. She must remember she really knew nothing about what kind of man he was— except, of course, that he had an adequate sperm count. Nor did she want to know. Instantly her defenses went back up.

"It's the letter I'm calling about," he said. "This

is awkward, but did you request me as a partner in your childbirth class?''

It was the last thing Megan had expected him to ask. ''No,'' she replied forcefully. ''Why would I do that?''

There was a pause. ''Could we get together somewhere and talk?'' he asked. ''It's hard to discuss this kind of thing over the phone.''

Panic welled in Megan. Everything was happening too fast. ''Getting together isn't a good idea. It's obvious the clinic made some kind of mistake, but we can still pretend we don't know each other's identity. I don't want anything from you, Mr. Duncan, and I don't want to meet you.'' Her voice was rising, so she took a deep breath. ''This was all supposed to be confidential. From here on out, let's keep it that way.''

Before he could reply, Megan hung up the receiver. She was shaking all over. This kind of stress couldn't be good for her baby. It sure as heck wasn't good for her. She ran a soothing hand over her stomach and murmured softly.

Before she could completely calm down, the phone rang again. Taking deep, slow breaths, she let the machine take it. Someone at the clinic had a lot of explaining to do! As soon as she heard Duncan's voice, she pressed her hands to her ears and left the room. Moving as quickly as she could, she went back upstairs, humming loudly to block him out.

The phone rang twice more that afternoon while

she tried to work. She thought about calling the clinic again, but she finally decided to wait until she'd had a chance to think the situation through. When she finally went back downstairs and saw the insistent flashing light on her answering machine, she deleted both messages without listening to them.

He called again while Megan was eating her supper—vegetable soup and a grilled cheese sandwich. She wasn't hungry, but her baby needed nourishment.

"Ms. Malone," his voice pleaded from her machine, "would you please pick up the phone? We need to talk. I'm not going to go away. Now that I know you're carrying my child, you can't expect me to just forget about it. I had no idea the clinic had used my sperm. They didn't have the right. It was a mistake, do you understand?"

A mistake? How could that be? Why would he donate sperm in the first place if he didn't want them to use it? She grabbed the receiver, intent on asking him just that.

"Oh, you're home," he said as soon as she identified herself.

Ignoring the trace of sarcasm in his voice, she asked about the mistake. "That *is* what happens when you donate to a fertility clinic," she added. He wasn't the only one who could be sarcastic.

He sighed. "Look, it's a long story, but I never agreed to be a part of the donor program. The first

I knew anything about this was when I got the letter today. If you don't believe me, ask the clinic staff.''

Megan chewed on her lip. ''I believe you,'' she said reluctantly. Why would he lie when she could find out the truth so easily? ''I already called, but no one there could tell me anything. I'll try again in the morning. They certainly have a lot of explaining to do about violating my confidentiality as well as yours.'' It must be an even bigger shock for him, she realized, finding out he'd fathered a child he hadn't planned on. ''I promise I won't ever bother you about this. Since you never intended to be a donor in the first place, you can just put the whole thing from your mind.''

''I don't think I can do that,'' he said slowly.

''What are you saying?'' Fresh panic sliced through her like a machete. ''You're not going to make trouble for me, are you? Sue the clinic if you need some kind of revenge.'' Men!

''A lawsuit wouldn't alter the fact that I'm going to be a father, that a child of mine is living a life I'll have no part of. I just don't think I can accept that as easily as you seem to expect me to.''

Megan squeezed her eyes shut. Going to be a father! This kind of talk wasn't what she wanted to hear. ''With or without your consent, you were a *donor*,'' she said. ''That's all. But I'm having this child alone, the way I've planned to do all along, and I'm raising it without any interference. As far as I'm concerned, you have no role here. You're not involved.''

"That's not true," he argued. "Now that I know about the baby, I can't pretend it doesn't exist."

"That's exactly what you must do," she insisted. "It's *my* baby and it's going to stay that way. I have a contract with the clinic. I requested an anonymous donor."

"You don't have a contract with me."

"Look," she said, "the sooner you accept the fact that you have no claim, the better off we'll both be." How she hoped that she was right about that! "Now I really have to go. Your complaint is with the clinic, not me."

If she had to, she would get an attorney and fight him, but she prayed it wouldn't come to that. She made a good living, but lawyers were expensive. No doubt it was Mr. Duncan's testosterone beating its chest over the situation, but when he really thought about the hassle, surely he'd lose interest.

Mac waited until the next day before he attempted to contact the birth mother again. Meanwhile, he tried without success to get in touch with someone at the clinic. Dennis hadn't gotten back yet and the director was still out sick. The receptionist's voice sounded panicky as she confided that things were a little confused right now and there was no one else who could help him at the moment.

Mac wanted to tell her that "confused" was putting it mildly.

"I'll definitely pass on your message as soon as I know who'll be filling in," she added.

''Good grief, how long is the director going to be gone?'' Mac demanded.

''I can't discuss that. All I can say is that she's ill, but as soon as I know who's handling her duties I'll have them call you.''

Frustrated, Mac gave up. Just his luck the clinic was apparently suffering some crisis of its own. Until he could get a few answers from them, he'd just have to deal with Megan Malone directly.

What was she like? He wondered. What kind of mother would she be? How well could she provide for the child? And what were Mac's obligations legally, financially and ethically? She might refuse his help, but that didn't let him off the hook, not as far as his own conscience was concerned. The more he thought about the situation, the more questions came up.

A baby needed a father, despite what this woman had said about raising it alone. Once she met him and saw for herself that he was a pretty normal guy and not a two-headed monster, she was bound to relent.

All Mac had to do was convince her to meet with him and talk over the situation. How hard could that be?

Chapter Two

The man was relentless. Megan fumed silently as she deleted yet another message from her answering machine. No one at the clinic would tell her anything about MacGregor Duncan. How ironic that they were suddenly so concerned with confidentiality.

"The man is the father of my baby," Megan had protested to some underling on the phone. "Thanks to your clinic's lack of discretion, I already have his name."

The person she needed to talk to was still unavailable and Megan's caustic comment had gotten her nowhere. Perhaps she would have to take Duncan's call after all. He'd certainly been persistent in the face of her unwavering rejection, making her wonder if he had the tenacity of a pit bull or was merely as dense as muffin batter that had been stirred too long. There was only one way to find out.

The next time Mac dialed the Malone woman's number, listened to her recorded greeting and identified himself, prepared to leave another message on her machine, she picked up the phone. He was so surprised that he nearly forgot what he was going to say, covering his momentary confusion with brusqueness.

"This class we're signed up for starts next week," he said. "We need to make some decisions."

"Don't worry about it," she replied, voice cool. "I still have time to find a partner."

"You mean you don't have anyone yet?" Mac demanded. Here was his opening, a way to get to know each other. "Does that mean you aren't married?"

"Why would it matter?" she countered. "Do you have something against single parents?"

Mac struggled for patience. "No, of course not. It just stands to reason that if you had a husband, he'd want to take the class with you."

"Oh. No, I'm not married." Her voice thawed a degree or two. "Are you?"

At least she was curious about him. "I'm involved with someone," he admitted, "but it won't be a problem."

"The class is two evenings a week, you know. That's a pretty big commitment for a busy man."

"I said my relationship won't be a problem." Mac hoped he was correct. How would Justine react to the news that another woman was having his child? They'd only been seeing each other for six months, but his parents were right. It was time he settled down and raised some little Duncans to carry on the family name.

"I was referring to your job, not your social life," Megan replied. "You do work, don't you?"

"Actually, I own a business, so my hours are flexible. Making time for the class wouldn't be a big deal." Perhaps he was pushing, but it seemed like the only way to stop her from shutting him out of his baby's life. If he allowed her to do that, he would always feel like part of him was missing.

The thought of his parents' reaction, if that happened and they found out, made him shudder.

When Megan didn't say anything, Mac tried a different tactic. "There's a part of me growing inside of you. We've made this baby together. Aren't you the least bit curious about me?"

"The clinic gave me all the information I needed when I picked you from the donor list," she said stubbornly, but he thought there was the tiniest hesitation in her voice.

"What did they tell you?" he asked, praying it

wasn't much. Even if she wasn't admitting it, she was bound to wonder.

"The description I read said that you're intelligent and attractive." Had her voice warmed a little more?

"Sounds accurate so far," he said lightly. "Did you see a photo?" He knew the answer. The clinic didn't have his picture.

"No, but I have a general description. Your looks weren't my first priority, Mr. Duncan."

"Call me Mac," he suggested. When she didn't reply, he forged on. "What are you going to tell our child about me? No kid wants its father to be a test tube."

"I haven't worked that all out yet," she said defensively. "I still have some time."

"But how will you answer the questions when they come?" Mac demanded. "The clinic can't have told you whether I played baseball or if I like vegetables, or even what kind of person I am. If you don't have the answers, our child will eventually be forced to go looking for them somewhere else. You'll lose any control over what he or she finds out. Is that what you want?"

"I hadn't thought about it," she admitted. "Maybe you could write a letter, one I could give him when he's old enough to understand the situation."

"Him?" Mac asked with a tremor in his voice he couldn't hide. Did she know the baby's sex already? Good God, was he going to have a son?

"I'm just guessing," she admitted. "They offered to tell me, but I don't want to know." For a moment there was silence on the line. "I think of him as a boy," she added softly. "It's probably silly."

The tenderness in her voice was nearly Mac's undoing. Hearing it was both reassuring and heart wrenching. At least she cared for the baby, but what was Mac supposed to do with *his* feelings? Forget them?

"So you know a little bit about me already, but I don't know anything about you except that you're pregnant with my baby," he said, gripping the receiver tighter. "Dammit, that's not good enough. I have rights, too."

As soon as the harsh words had left his mouth, he realized he'd made a big mistake. He was met with a wall of silence. "Can't you put yourself in my place?" he pleaded, the effort to lower his voice nearly closing off his throat. "If our roles were reversed, wouldn't you want to know something about the person who was going to be raising your firstborn? Wouldn't you?"

"It wasn't supposed to be like this," she cried. "I don't know why you donated sperm and I don't care, but if you don't stop harassing me, I'll report you. I'll get an attorney if I have to. Leave me alone!"

Before Mac could say anything more, she crashed the receiver down in his ear.

Hell, he'd really blown it with his *Me, Tarzan, you, Jane* routine.

Before he could think what to do next, the door to his office flew open and one of his men poked his head through the doorway. "Boss, the windows for the Merritt project just came in and we have a little problem," Archer said, tugging on the bill of his Broncos cap. "Can you take a look?"

Just what he needed—something else to deal with.

"Can't you handle it?" he demanded.

Archer's eyes widened. "I don't think so, but I guess I can try."

Instantly ashamed of his outburst, Mac muttered an apology. "Show me the problem." Putting aside his frustration, he followed the younger man out to the large shop where most of the work was done on the custom playhouses they manufactured. This project was a rush job, a birthday surprise for the daughter of a computer guru out on the coast. Like nearly everything Mac's company created, the playhouse was a miniature reproduction of the family home, right down to the front porch columns and the dormer windows. It was being designed and built in sections here in Buttonwood, using blueprints of the bigger house as well as photos and videotapes. Once the playhouse was finished, it would be shipped and assembled on location.

The windows were one of the few parts that weren't custom-made at Mac's plant. Instead they were manufactured by an outfit in Denver.

As soon as he saw them, he recognized the problem. The French doors for the back of the playhouse were supposed to be framed in oak, exactly like those in the main house. Instead they'd been stained a dark walnut color.

"I'll call Mountain View," he told Archer. "There's still time for them to redo the order and express it before our deadline."

Archer looked relieved as he maneuvered the toothpick in his mouth from one side to the other. Like the other employees, he had worked with Mac for nearly ten years, since Mac had taken Small World from a hobby to a full-time business and moved it to Buttonwood. Before that, Archer had been a house framer with a local construction company.

Mac could still remember with painful clarity his parents' reaction when he'd announced that he was quitting his job as an architect with a major Denver firm to build playhouses. To say they had disapproved would be a serious understatement. They were sure he'd lost his mind.

It hadn't been the first time they were disappointed in their only offspring. Given his track record as a dutiful son, neither would it be the last.

"I'll let you deal with Charlie," Archer said. "I've got a balcony railing to put together." His tool belt jingled as he walked away.

Mac returned to his office and looked up Charlie's number at Mountain View. As Mac had known he would, the window manufacturer promised to make up the correct doors and send them right away. Another crisis averted. If only all of Mac's problems were this easy to solve.

Megan pushed the cart through the produce section of the local grocery store, glancing at her short list of items before she stopped to pick out a plump, radiant tomato. Since her pregnancy, she'd been making a concerted effort to eat healthy. She walked every day, avoided caffeine and took her prenatal vitamins.

The third bedroom of her town home had already been turned into a nursery, its walls painted a cheerful yellow. In her mind she could picture the wallpaper border that matched the curtains she'd sewn herself. A new crib sat next to a matching dresser filled with baby clothes and supplies. In the closet was a safety-approved baby seat for the car. The only thing Megan hadn't planned on providing for her child was a daddy.

Blindly, she steered her cart toward the seafood counter, replaying her conversation with Mac Duncan in her head as she dodged a little girl pushing a miniature stroller.

If our roles were reversed, he'd said, *wouldn't you want to know something about the person who was going to raise your firstborn?*

Was Megan being unreasonable in refusing to let him into her life? She hadn't thought so when she put down the phone, but now she couldn't help but wonder. How would she feel if the shoe was on the other foot?

To have a child out there somewhere, not knowing how it was treated, what it was being taught or even whether it was loved would be the worst pain she could imagine. Countless women who'd given up their babies for one reason or another had to live with that uncertainty. Did Megan have the right to make this man endure that same torture?

Her hand drifted to her abdomen. Whatever Mr. Duncan's reason for donating sperm, he had in essence given her this child. Did that grant her the right to keep it from him or was she just being selfish?

Megan's breath caught as an idea took root.

Perhaps all he really wanted was reassurance. Once he was convinced that she was a normal, caring person who would be a good mother to this baby, maybe his conscience would be satisfied and he'd just go away.

As Megan swung her cart around a corner, excitement coursing through her, she narrowly missed running into Blanche Hastings, one of the town busybodies.

"Well, hello, honey," Blanche said, her gaze darting to Megan's stomach. "How's our little mother doing?"

Megan forced a smile. She suspected that Blanche and her friend, Flo Harris, weren't above gossiping about Megan's pregnancy and her lack of a husband. They prided themselves on knowing everything that went on in town.

"I'm just fine," Megan replied politely as she maneuvered her cart around Blanche's. "And you?"

"Right as rain, and glad winter's finally over. Are you getting ready for the blessed event?"

"Sure am." Megan didn't want to get stuck answering any probing questions like the last time she'd run into Blanche and Flo. Lucky for Megan, another of their friends had appeared and she'd been able to make her escape without responding.

"We'll have to throw you a shower," Blanche said now, eagle eyes sharp as she assessed Megan's tummy. "When are you due?"

"That's so sweet of you." Megan's smile felt stiff. "There's still plenty of time, though." The last thing she wanted was to be the center of attention in a roomful of women speculating about her circumstances. "I'll get back to you, okay?"

Before Blanche could fire off another awkward question, Megan stuck out her arm and glanced at her watch with exaggerated horror. "Goodness, I have an appointment in a little bit," she said apologetically, mental fingers crossed. "Sorry, but I have to run." Without a backward glance, she hurried down the next aisle.

Too bad there wasn't someone whose advice she could seek in what to do about Duncan, but she had no family with whom she kept in close touch. Although she'd made a few friends since moving here and a couple of them knew the circumstances behind her pregnancy, this wasn't something she felt comfortable discussing with any of them. The decision was hers alone, and it was one she would have to make very soon, despite what she'd told Blanche.

Biting her lower lip, she plucked a bag of peanut butter M&M's from the shelf. There was good health, and then there was quality of life, she reasoned as she headed for the pasta aisle. Hoping she was correct about assuaging the man's curiosity, she made her decision.

"I've reconsidered."

It seemed that every time Mac heard Megan's voice, he was so surprised by it that he nearly dropped the phone. Since he'd last talked to her, he'd been swamped with the Merritt project at work, frustrated with the clinic's continued evasiveness and curiously reluctant to seek legal advice from a family friend in Denver. Cooperation was always preferable to adversity, and he still hoped to resolve the issue between Megan and himself peaceably.

He'd talked to Dennis briefly and the other man had promised to look into the situation and call Mac back, which he hadn't done yet.

Unfortunately Mac was leaving for Atlanta first thing in the morning to attend a huge trade show. The convention usually provided a few solid leads and he wasn't about to forgo the trip while he waited for Dennis's call.

"What exactly do you mean by reconsidered?" he asked her now in a cautious voice. Was she finally willing to listen to reason?

She blew out a breath. "You're right. If our situations were reversed, I'd want to know what kind of person was raising my child," she admitted.

Relief pumped through him. "Taking that class together would give us a chance to get to know each other," he suggested, his mind leaping ahead. "It starts on Tuesday."

To his astonishment, she didn't immediately object. "I think we should have a face-to-face meeting before then," she said instead.

"I'd like that, too. Unfortunately I'm leaving town first thing in the morning and I won't be back until late the afternoon of the first class." Mac felt genuine regret. What if they loathed each other on sight? "I'd postpone the trip if I could, but it's too important." Would she think his priorities were out of whack? That he should put the child ahead of everything else? He refrained from pointing out that her own stubbornness was the reason they'd run out of time.

Megan gripped the receiver tighter, still clinging to the hope that he'd lose interest in the class and in her soon enough. She couldn't imagine him giving up two evenings a week for a stranger and a child he'd fathered with so little involvement. If she was wrong about his staying power she'd be stuck with him for the duration, but if she wasn't and he did drop out, she would probably be allowed to continue the course without a partner, since her due date was so near.

The idea cheered her. She was tired of arguing, tired of dodging him. And it wasn't as though she'd lined up anyone else to go with her. If the truth be told, she hadn't even asked around.

"What time are you leaving on your trip?" Perhaps they could still meet before then.

"Early. My flight out of Denver is at eight, so I'll have to catch the first commuter plane from the county airport."

Megan groaned softly. She wasn't a morning person at the best of times, but now that she was pregnant, getting up at dawn wasn't a sacrifice she was willing to make. "Okay," she said on a burst of bravado. "If you're sure you want to go through with this, I guess I'll see you at the center on Tuesday evening."

"How will I know you?" he asked.

"I'll be the pregnant one," she quipped, suddenly nervous. What was she getting herself into?

He chuckled appreciatively at her lame attempt at humor. "Oh, sure, I hadn't thought of that."

"Actually, my hair is kind of long and dark blonde," she said, gesturing with her free hand even though he couldn't see. "I'll be wearing jeans and a red top."

"And you'll be alone," he added with typical

masculine bluntness. "I mean, everyone else should be paired up with someone."

Megan pressed a hand to her stomach, seeking reassurance. "That's right, two by two, just like on Noah's Ark." This was a huge mistake. She just knew it. "And I already have a description of you."

"Yeah, I remember." His tone was dry. "Intelligent and attractive. I'll do my best to live up to that."

As soon as she hung up, Megan realized that she had completely forgotten to talk to him about ground rules. He needed to understand that just because she'd agreed to take the class with him didn't mean he was horning into her life.

Mac glanced at his watch as he drove into the clinic parking lot. Of course the plane from Atlanta had been late, and then an unexpected blizzard at the supposedly blizzard-proof Denver airport delayed his commuter flight. Despite all that, it was barely six-thirty. He had hoped to arrive a few minutes early so he could catch his breath and introduce himself to Megan before class began, but at least he wasn't going to be so late that he made a bad first impression.

While he was in Atlanta he'd talked to Dennis Reid again. The chief of staff had spent the first five minutes of their conversation bragging about his new girlfriend, a "gorgeous babe" named Rachel, until Mac finally interrupted.

"Sorry to cut this short, but I've got an appointment in a few minutes. Were you able to find out anything about my situation?''

On the other end of the line, Dennis cleared his throat and Mac's heart sank. Bad news.

''Truth is, I haven't learned a thing, buddy. The director's had major surgery, very unexpected. Then there was a big computer crash. Between you and me, the place is in chaos. Not my department, you understand, but the admin side's a mess. Like a ship without a rudder. Until they sort things out, it's not a time to get answers. Wish I had better news.''

Swallowing his frustration, Mac had thanked Dennis for his time and promised to get together for racquetball the next week. Maybe by then Dennis would have found out something for him.

Now Mac pulled his pickup into a parking slot and hurried inside the clinic, following the bright pink signs down the empty hallway. At the far end he could see a small group of people going two by two into one of the rooms. Slightly apart from the rest stood a woman with her back to Mac. She was wearing red and her hair was a tangle of dark honey.

Megan.

As he walked quickly toward her, his footsteps echoing in the hall, she turned around. Some part of Mac's brain noticed that she was attractive despite her serious expression. The rest of him was too busy staring at the bulge beneath her red blouse.

She was a lot farther along than he'd imagined, her body swollen with his child.

His child.

The enormity of it drove the air out of him like a hard fist to the gut. He faltered, his legs suddenly shaky, knowing he was gawking but unable to stop. Somehow hearing about the baby's existence hadn't even begun to prepare him for the visual.

"Are you Mac?" Her voice was low, betraying nothing, but her hands were linked in front of her, fingers poker straight. He wasn't the only nervous one here.

The other people had already gone inside, leaving him and this woman alone in the hall.

"Yeah, I'm Mac Duncan," he croaked. "And you're Megan. Hi."

He must have sounded normal enough to appease her. After a barely perceptible hesitation, she stuck out her hand. Her full mouth relaxed its pinched expression as she studied him, but when he touched her fingers, they were icy cold.

Wanting to stare at the evidence of her pregnancy, he forced himself instead to focus on her face. Her cheeks were gently flushed and her eyes were hazel. He must have looked as dazed as he felt, because a tiny crease appeared between her brows.

"Hi," she echoed. "I was beginning to think you'd changed your mind."

Vaguely he remembered the time. "I'd hoped to be here a few minutes early," he said apologetically, "but the Denver airport's a mess. It's snowing there."

She looked surprised. "Well, at least you're here now."

Feeling awkward, Mac ran a hand through his short brown hair. It was probably standing on end. He'd meant to shave in the car, but his razor was packed and he hadn't wanted to take the time to pull over and dig it out. Some impression he must make—running late, with rumpled clothes and a five o'clock shadow.

Megan, on the other hand, looked neat and pretty despite her extremely rounded figure. Mac hadn't thought to ask on the phone when she was due. "How far along are you?" he blurted.

The blush on her cheeks deepened as she plucked at her blouse. He hadn't meant to embarrass her. Good manners had been drilled into him at an early age, but he had no idea what the protocol was for this particular situation.

"I'm due a month from yesterday," she replied with a gesture toward the open door. "I think we'd probably better go in."

From the expression on Mac Duncan's attractive face, Megan could see that her appearance had been a shock. Had he expected her to be prettier, younger or just thinner? Was he disappointed? The way he'd gaped at her stomach made Megan feel as though she were carrying quintuplets in a wheelbarrow.

Too bad, because he made her wish, just for a moment, that she was available and unencumbered.

He was a very attractive man. No doubt the hot flash that engulfed her had more to do with her hormone level than his great cheekbones or his sexy mouth, but having a child who looked like him would be no great hardship.

The rest of the class was waiting for them. As soon as Mac followed her inside, the instructor shut the door behind them.

''Welcome to 'We're Having a Baby,''' the woman said with a smile as Megan hurried over to a couple of empty chairs at the edge of the group, near a pile of mats and pillows. Her footsteps echoed loudly on the vinyl floor. Being the center of attention always made her uncomfortable.

''I'm Dr. Claire Davis,'' the instructor continued, ''and from the number of maternity outfits I see, you all appear to be in the right place.''

The five other women and their partners chuckled appreciatively while Mac sat down next to Megan.

''I'm a pediatrician here at the clinic,'' the doctor continued. She was a slim, pretty woman with dark red hair, blue eyes and a warm smile. Megan wondered if Mac found Dr. Davis attractive. ''Several of us on the medical staff are assigned to these classes on a rotating schedule.'' She picked up a clipboard and glanced at it. ''I'll be your instructor for the next six weeks and we'll all be working together closely, so please call me Claire. Now it's your turn to introduce yourselves. Tell us whatever you'd like everyone to know.'' She glanced at Mac and Megan. ''Let's start with you.''

Wondering if anyone else here had gone the artificial insemination route, Megan stood up and gave her name. As she glanced at the others, all paired off and smiling, she felt like the only girl at the dance without a date.

"And who's this with you?" the doctor prompted gently.

Megan glanced at the man standing beside her, but her mind went blank. Someone giggled. He shifted closer, his hand curling warmly around hers.

"I guess she's forgotten," he teased, the twinkle in his eyes taking away any possible sting as a smile tugged at his mouth. "You'd think we just met."

Megan stiffened. Was he going to pretend that they, too, were a couple, or spill the beans and humiliate her?

His dark eyes seemed to say "trust me." Fingers laced with hers, he introduced himself to the group. "We live right here in town," he added.

She knew he was only playing a role, but for the first time since she'd made her decision to have this child, she felt like part of a team. This time when he grinned at her, she managed to smile back at him.

"Are you the father?" asked a girl who looked barely old enough to be pregnant.

"Let's not ask personal questions," the doctor interjected. "We'll volunteer what we'd like the group to know." She glanced back at Mac and Megan, but neither spoke again.

Megan wondered if anyone could tell that they barely knew each other. She certainly wasn't ashamed of the method she had used to become pregnant, but neither was she eager to justify herself to a room full of happy couples.

"Well, thank you," the doctor said after a moment. "We have a lot of material to cover tonight, so let's move on."

The two of them sat back down and Megan disentangled herself from Mac's grip. "Thanks," she murmured. "I'm not usually so inept."

"No problem." He shifted slightly away from her. Apparently she'd been right that his show of unity had been just that, an act for the others. Wasn't that what she wanted—her independence? Before she could sort through her feelings, another couple, both wearing rings, stood up and began talking excitedly.

There were a dozen people in all, including a mother and daughter, another pair who appeared to be platonic friends, a man and woman who kept touching each other and exchanging smoldering glances, and two married couples each having their first baby. None of the other women were as big as Megan.

Glancing at the wall clock, Claire explained what they would be covering in class. "Tonight we're going to talk about breathing and relaxation techniques to use during labor and delivery. We'll spread out the mats and go over a few simple positions that will keep you comfortable as your pregnancies progress,'' she said. ''While you're practicing, I'll discuss your baby's development.'' She pulled down a chart that showed the stages of the fetus's growth in living color.

Megan didn't look at Mac, but she wondered whether he was having second thoughts yet. The huge colored photographs had to be more than he'd bargained for.

''Next time we'll tour the labor ward,'' Claire continued. ''Later on we'll also cover the Lamaze and Bradley methods of childbirth, the stages of labor, some visualization techniques, the various kinds of anesthetics and how they're administered, unexpected events, postpartum recovery and infant care.'' She glanced around the room. ''We'll review bottle feeding, bathing the newborn and diaper-changing. There will be plenty of time for questions and discussion, so don't hold back.''

When no one said anything, she directed them to select from the pile of mats and pillows. Feeling awkward, Megan followed her instruction to lie down while Mac knelt beside her.

''Are you comfortable?'' he asked in an undertone as Claire described what she wanted them to do.

Comfortable? Megan felt like the proverbial beached whale who'd washed up at the feet of an extremely attractive beachcomber. If their baby was a boy, she hoped he looked like his father.

''I'm okay,'' she stammered when she realized

Mac was waiting for an answer. When had she started thinking of this as *their* baby?

Mac was watching her with a concerned frown, so she did her best to give him a reassuring smile although she felt very awkward when Claire urged them to use the pillows to try the different positions she was describing.

"As your weight increases, you'll need to make more adjustments," she said. Her glance at Megan was sympathetic, making her feel even more clumsy. She must look as ridiculous as she felt.

Mac was glad when the exercise was over and he could get to his feet. Trying to help Megan shift and turn on the mat had been an awkward experience, considering that they barely knew each other and he was never quite sure where to touch her.

From the pink in her cheeks, he assumed she found their situation equally uncomfortable. Perhaps this had all been a big mistake. In the week since he'd gotten the letter from the clinic, he'd thought a lot about what he was getting into.

Now he took Megan's hand and carefully helped her to her feet. Their eyes met and that intriguing splash of color ran up her cheeks again. She looked away, but not before Mac heard her sharply indrawn breath. No doubt the baby was crowding her lungs or something equally clinical.

Claire called for a short break. There was a general exodus from the room and Megan's gaze followed the others.

"I need to, um, use the restroom," she said softly. "Pregnancy does that."

"I'll walk you out," Mac replied. "Maybe there's a coffee machine somewhere. Want some?"

She shook her head. "Caffeine's bad for the baby. I'd better get in line."

Feeling like an idiot, he watched her leave the room.

"How's it going?" Claire asked him when everyone else was gone.

"I just realized how little I know about this," he admitted.

"The class?" she asked with a chuckle. "That's why you're here."

"No, the whole deal about having a child," he replied, wondering how much she had been told.

Claire patted his arm and smiled. "You're not alone," she said. "First time father?"

"Yeah, that's me." Just saying it made him feel good. A foolish grin spread across his face.

"The best thing you can do is to talk to your partner," Claire suggested. "There's no better way to share in the experience than communication. And be sure to ask questions while you're here. No matter how trivial it may seem, you'll only be putting into words what someone else is wondering about, too."

Before he could thank her for the advice, three of the women came back. They were laughing and he heard the words "potty breaks" and "shrinking bladder'' before he saw Megan trail after them. He remembered Claire's words.

"Would you like to stop somewhere afterwards?'' he asked Megan when she joined him. They needed to talk.

Her gaze was guarded. "What for?''

"How about ice cream?'' he asked. "With hotfudge topping?''

"You make it hard to say no,'' she admitted with a slight smile.

Relieved, Mac cupped her elbow. "That was my intention.'' If he had his way, she would agree to everything he suggested.

Chapter Three

It was all Megan could do to wait for Mac to slide into the red vinyl booth across from her before she dug into her sundae. They'd agreed to meet at the Dairy Freeze near the clinic, where he had insisted on paying for her ice cream along with his own. Ordinarily that kind of macho taking-care-of-the-little-woman gesture set her teeth on edge, but he'd done it with a wink that made her feel more like an attractive female than an overweight incubator.

"Humor me," he'd pleaded, as if he understood that she was used to paying her own way. Refusing would have been churlish.

Now he took a bite of his banana split as she ate a mouthful of ice cream and closed her eyes in sheer bliss. The creamy sweetness exploded on her tongue and slid down her throat like a sigh.

How had he known she'd been fighting a major chocolate craving all day? She'd given up caffeine and alcohol, and she watched what she ate, but in the last eight months chocolate had become an obsession. Because of those first insistent cravings, she'd suspected she might be pregnant even before she'd used the home test.

When she opened her eyes, he was watching her with blatant curiosity. Embarrassed, Megan looked away as an old song about a teen angel spun around them. The Dairy Freeze was decorated with fifties memorabilia, including miniature jukeboxes at each booth and black vinyl records—45s—scattered over the walls.

"This is pretty good," Mac said of his ice cream, breaking the awkward silence between them. "Thanks for agreeing to come with me."

"Thanks for asking." Megan licked fudge sauce from her spoon, sneaking peeks at him as he continued to study her openly. His interest spiked her temperature. She liked his weathered face. His dark, compelling eyes were fringed with lashes any woman would kill for. His hair was a warm brown, combed off his wide forehead and cut nearly short enough to disguise its tendency to wave. With luck, his genes would breed true.

He oozed masculinity and she had his undivided attention. Just because she was as big as a house didn't mean she couldn't appreciate the company of a handsome man. Too darned bad he was only assessing her as breeding stock.

Under his prolonged scrutiny she began to wonder whether her mascara had smudged or she sported a smear of chocolate on her chin. What did he think of her?

"I know nothing about you," he said finally as the wailing ballad was replaced by energetic surfer music that made Megan want to tap her foot. "What do I ask first?"

Not sure how to reply, she shoveled in more ice cream. "What do you want to know?" she asked, mouth full.

"Why don't you tell me why you're having this baby." He certainly cut to the chase. "Your pregnancy wasn't an accident. It had to be something you planned, but you don't have a husband to share the responsibility."

"And I don't need one," she said defensively. "I've never been married." Now why had she volunteered that? "I wanted a baby and I'm perfectly capable of raising it alone." What right did this man, this would-be anonymous donor, have to question her decision? There was no reason for her to justify it, not to him.

"What about your girlfriend?" she asked above the escalating drumbeat from the jukebox. "How does she feel about you being a donor to another woman?" Unless she was made of ice or didn't really care about him, that had to hurt.

His mouth tightened. "I didn't intend for the clinic to use my sperm." He ignored the way her eyes must have widened in disbelief. "Before I started seeing Justine, I went to the clinic to help out a friend."

"She must be some friend," Megan drawled.

Mac's cheeks darkened at her comment. "She was single and she wanted a baby. I guess *you* could understand that feeling?" His brows lifted sardonically.

Megan flushed at his tone. "Maybe. Why don't you just go on with your story."

"She changed her mind about the baby and now she's married to a great guy. They'll probably have their own family."

One of the lucky ones, Megan thought.

"Unfortunately by the time I tried to inform the clinic that my donation was no longer needed, it was too late. The rest, as they say, is history." His gaze flicked downward to where the table hid her stomach. "I still haven't gotten an explanation from them for what happened."

Megan sat back in the booth. Behind her a little boy began to bang his spoon on the table and whimper. She could hear his daddy attempting to soothe him. "And Justine?" she asked. "She's okay with this?"

Mac ran a hand through his hair. On one finger was a ring with a dark red stone. His file said he was college educated. She'd have to ask about his major. "I have no idea how Justine feels. I haven't told her."

Megan frowned. What kind of man would keep something that important from the woman in his life? "Your relationship can't be very serious," she said without thinking.

To her surprise, instead of telling her to mind her own business, he merely shrugged as he considered the question. "A week ago I would have said it was, but now I don't know. Don't get me wrong, she's a nice woman." He spread his hands in a helpless gesture. "It's complicated."

Megan hoped his complications had nothing to do with her baby. The last thing she wanted was for him to make any major changes because of this situation. Unlike hers, his entire life wasn't going to revolve around the child. How did she come right out and caution him not to expect more from her than she was willing to allow? If she was wrong, she'd look like a fool and embarrass them both.

Perhaps it was time for a change of subject. "Tell me about your parents," she suggested. "Are you a native?" She would have liked to ask how much interference she could expect from his side of the family. On second thought, it might be nice for her baby to have grandparents.

"I grew up in Denver," he replied. "My parents still live there. How about you? Born and raised in Buttonwood?"

Megan remembered all the places she'd lived as a child, staying with a relative until she became an inconvenience and was shuffled to another like an unwanted package. A shiver of reaction went through her.

"I moved around a lot," she admitted reluctantly, "but I've lived here for three years. I like the small-town atmosphere."

She didn't add that one of the things that had drawn her to Buttonwood was the fertility clinic. After several relationships that went nowhere, she'd finally figured out if she wanted to have a family, it was up to her to do something about it. She had gotten tired of waiting for the right man to come along and get her with child.

The Buttonwood Baby Clinic had seemed perfect for her needs, but she'd thought long and hard about taking such a momentous step, even after she had settled here. The way the clinic had botched the confidentiality issue had shaken her faith in that institution, but she was trying to keep an open mind until she got an explanation. If she ever did.

"You haven't really answered my other question," he reminded her. "Why do this now, while you're on your own?"

His meaning was clear. "Lots of single women have children," she said defensively.

His gaze remained steady. "And I respect them for it, but they don't all go to the lengths you did to become pregnant."

Her chin lifted. "It was my choice to make and I'm happy with it."

He must have realized he wasn't gaining any points by quizzing her, because he pressed his lips into a firm line as if he were holding back more questions.

From a nearby booth came a burst of masculine laughter. Two young couples were crowded into it, talking loudly. For a moment Megan envied them, and then she remembered her own adolescence. She'd never been like that—carefree, confident, bold enough to want attention.

Mac, too, glanced at the teens. "Do you work here in town?" Megan asked after he turned back around. When he'd pulled up beside her at the Dairy Freeze earlier, she had noticed some lettering on the door of his truck, but she hadn't read it. He was tanned, even this early in the year, as though he spent a lot of time outdoors. Maybe he was a skier. Megan had tackled the bunny slopes on a few occasions, but she was far from competent. Or perhaps he worked construction. Considering the width of his shoulders and chest, he looked strong enough for physical labor.

"I own a local company called Small World," he said. "We build playhouses."

"Children's playhouses?" she blurted.

His grin was resigned, as if he'd been asked the same question before. "Yeah, that's right. Each one is custom designed, usually to duplicate the family home—on a much smaller scale, of course. I'll have to show you some pictures of what we've done."

Megan mulled that over. When she'd stayed with her aunt, there had been a dirty, abandoned chicken coop next door. Megan had pretended it was a playhouse until the neighbor caught her and complained.

"That sounds like a pretty cool job," she told Mac, "but you must travel a lot." How much demand would there be for custom playhouses in a town the size of Buttonwood, population 75,000?

"Some," he admitted. "We have customers all over the country, and I cover a few exhibitions, but we do the actual planning and construction of each playhouse right here in town." He poked at his melting ice cream with his spoon. "I'll give you a tour."

It was a throwaway line, like "let's do lunch."

"Sure," she said, hardly able to resist scraping the leftover fudge sauce from the sides of her sundae dish bowl. What was it about chocolate? At home she'd stashed bowls of candy in strategic places. "It sounds like a fun job," she conceded.

"It has its moments. How about you?" he asked. "Do you work?"

Did he think she was independently wealthy, having a child to relieve her boredom? "I index cookbooks." Few people had any idea what that meant. From Mac's puzzled expression, he was in the majority. "I edit the text and set up the index for the back of the book, so people can locate all the recipes for salmon or squash," she explained.

His frown cleared. "Yeah, I know what you mean. I guess I figured whoever wrote the book did the index, too."

"That's what most people think, but it's a separate skill."

"Do you work for a local company?" he asked, managing to look interested.

"No, I freelance for several publishers on a regular basis. It's all done by mail. I have a computer in my home office and I set my own hours.'' That was the part most people envied, never realizing the discipline it took to stay on schedule or how many distractions there were working at home.

''You must be a very organized person.'' His astuteness surprised her.

''I haven't always been,'' she confessed. ''But with a baby coming, I'm getting better. I figured I'd have to.''

Abruptly Mac leaned forward. ''I've thought about our baby a lot since I got that letter. I'm not sure just how we'll work it out yet, but I want to play a real part in my child's life.''

For a moment, his smile distracted her, and then the meaning behind his words sank in. ''What exactly are you telling me?'' she asked, warning flags popping up like spring bulbs.

''You don't have to raise this baby alone.'' He looked pleased with his announcement.

Megan didn't share his satisfaction. She gripped the edge of the table as a chill slid down her spine. He was still a stranger. ''I have every intention of doing just that,'' she pointed out.

Her declaration bunched his dark brows into a frown. ''What are you afraid of? We both want what's best for our child.''

Our child! ''I'm not afraid of anything,'' she retorted. Honesty compelled her to add, ''The idea of meeting you is still a new one for me. If it wasn't for that letter, we wouldn't even be having this conversation.''

Mac looked thoughtful. ''Yeah, I suppose you're

right. I've been talking to the chief of staff at the clinic, Dennis Reid, but he hasn't found anything out yet. Apparently the director had emergency surgery. Add some glitch with the computer system and everything's been a mess ever since.''

''They should have some kind of backup plan,'' she said, annoyed. ''Think of the records that could be jeopardized.''

''No kidding.'' His tone was dry.

''Why did you contact the chief of staff?'' she asked. ''Do you know him?'' She'd never met the man, but she'd probably seen the name on some clinic directory.

''Yeah, we play racquetball.''

No wonder Mac appeared to be in such good shape. ''Do you ski?'' she asked.

He shrugged. ''My parents are into it and I learned while I was growing up, but I don't have much time for it anymore. Do you?''

''Not well.'' She grinned. ''And not lately.''

His answering smile was dazzling. ''We'll have to teach junior to ski,'' he said.

The image of the three of them was a tempting fantasy to Megan, who had longed for a family of her own. She had to remind herself that Mac was only here because of the baby, not to forge some cozy relationship with her. His intentions might be sincere, his enthusiasm high at the moment, but who knew what the future would bring? Had he really thought about the long years involved in raising a child? It wouldn't be smart to count on him too much.

"I'm not thinking that far ahead," she said firmly.

"That's understandable." Did he realize she still had serious doubts about him? He struck her as a man who always got what he went after. What if what he wanted this time was her baby?

Panic hit, followed closely by a wave of exhaustion. She glanced at her watch, surprised by how late it was. She needed more sleep than usual and the added stress she'd been dealing with these last few days was starting to take its toll. She smothered a yawn.

"Tired?" Mac reached over to pat her free hand. His fingers were callused, but his touch was unbelievably warm. Startled by her vulnerability, she eased away from him on the pretense of shifting her purse. This wasn't the time to start leaning on anyone. "It's past my bedtime," she explained. "Expectant mothers need more sleep."

His expression cleared. "Of course, I nearly forgot—" He broke off abruptly.

What had he been about to say, that her pregnancy had slipped his mind? Not likely. He was probably referring to some of the side effects Claire had mentioned in class. Exhaustion, moodiness, insomnia, increased or diminished libido. She'd blushed at that one, but Mac hadn't appeared to notice.

"Ready?" he asked now. When she nodded, he slid from the booth and held out his hand.

Megan considered pretending not to notice. The attraction she felt toward him would only complicate things. Then she decided a woman in her condition needed her thrills, too. She allowed him to help her to her feet and grimaced as she tried to maneuver herself out of the confined area of the booth.

His gaze dropped to her stomach and he swallowed, looking suddenly apprehensive.

"I'm not going into labor just yet," she said with a sniff. "You don't have to get nervous."

His grin flashed and she had to stifle a sigh of response. "It shows? I'm trying to be stoic, but this is all pretty new stuff. I don't have much experience with kids."

Not knowing how to reply, Megan headed for the exit. Mac followed her out to her car as she wondered how wide her butt looked from the back. Digging out her keys and facing him, she felt as awkward as if she were bidding a blind date goodnight.

"Thanks for the sundae," she said. "I guess I'll see you at class, unless you've changed your mind?" The question came out sounding more hopeful than she'd intended. Well, she refused to hide her feelings. She hadn't wanted him involved and she wasn't entirely convinced this was a good idea. He'd have to deal with that.

Mac surprised her by gently capturing her wrists. "You aren't going to lose me this easily," he said, drawing her closer, "so you might as well get used to my presence in your life." Then he startled her even more by leaning down and kissing her cheek.

The brief touch of his lips was warm and his cologne, something spicy, teased her senses.

"Accept it, Megan," he said, voice husky as he straightened and released her. "I'm sticking. We're in this together."

Going down the long driveway to his house, side window open to the crisp night air, Mac heard Rusty start to bark from the big backyard. Although it was surrounded by a tall wood fence, the dog knew the sound of Mac's truck. Archer, who'd been dog-sitting, had probably dropped the Irish Setter off on his way home from work.

For a moment after Mac killed the engine, he rested his hands on the steering wheel and admired his house in the golden glow of the porch light. It was an old-fashioned place with two stories and a deep porch. Over the double front doors was a hexagon-shaped window that let in morning light. When Mac had first seen the house it sat vacant and neglected, but for several years now he'd been slowly restoring and remodeling it. He was a long way from finished, but the outside, at least, looked pretty respectable.

Set back from the road and fronted by a slightly rolling lawn, it was painted light-blue-gray. The shutters and trim were white to match the picket fence across the front and the door was navy with bright brass trim. Narrowing his gaze, Mac tried to picture a child playing on the grass.

Mac sighed. Tonight he was too tired to pick through his feelings and impressions. He knew only that the day he'd opened that letter, his life had shifted in a way he'd never imagined.

Rusty barked again, no doubt impatient to say hello. "Easy, boy, I'm coming," Mac called. He rolled up the window and grabbed his bag from behind the seat. The property surrounding his house might be generous, but that didn't mean the neighbors couldn't hear Rusty's effusive greeting.

As soon as Mac unlatched the gate, the dog's wiggling body burst out of the enclosure. His excited barking slurred into eager whines.

Talking softly, Mac squatted down and ruffled Rusty's dark red coat. There was something to be said for the unconditional, uncomplicated love of man's best friend, he thought with wry amusement.

"Did you miss me? Were you good?" Mac asked as the dog's wet tongue swiped his cheek. "Did you have fun with Archer's collie?"

Rusty whined again, crowding close as Mac caressed his silky head and fondled his floppy ears. Taking advantage of Mac's crouched position, the dog jumped up and sent him sprawling onto the grass.

"Okay, okay," he said with a chuckle, dodging the long pink tongue. Damn, but he was tired. Maybe he'd just lie here for a few minutes. The grass was soft and the cool air was refreshing. It had been a long day, meetings in Atlanta in the morning, two flights home, the dash back to Buttonwood for the class and then Megan.

Rusty finally hunkered down beside him as he stared up at the stars twinkling through the streaky clouds. For the first time since Megan had asked about Justine, he thought of her and felt guilty for not calling as he'd promised he would. It was too late now. She did the early news on a local cable show, so she was probably asleep.

A shiver went through Mac as the night air finally chilled him and he got to his feet. He walked toward the house with Rusty padding patiently beside him. He'd take her to dinner tomorrow to make up for his neglect, he decided, and they'd talk. There was a lot he needed to say.

The day after the first baby class, Megan sat at her desk and opened the latest packet from one of the publishers she worked for on a regular basis. Inside were the pages of a new dessert cookbook, including the illustrations.

Just what she needed, exposure to chocolate. Automatically her hand reached out to the bowl of M&M's beside the phone as she frowned at the treadmill sitting in the middle of the room like an instrument of torture.

Cassius was asleep on his carpeted perch in the window. In addition to the L-shaped desk with its computer and ergonomic keyboard, Megan's office contained a printer and a fax machine, a couple of file cabinets and two walls of bookshelves that went all the way to the ceiling. They held her growing collection of out-of-print and rare cookbooks as well as her reference section. There were books about spices, vegetables, fruits, diets and nutrition. Below them were a group of foreign language dictionaries and an international culinary dictionary. Ethnic recipes were popular and Megan had to know what the unfamiliar words in each title meant before she could properly index them. Another shelf held cookbooks she had previously worked on, in case she needed to double-check a particular publisher's style preference.

There was a wastebasket, a recycling bin for paper, a cabinet full of office supplies, a desk lamp and a wall calendar with pictures of cats. The room contained nearly everything Megan needed for her job. Despite the millions of recipes that had already been printed in thousands of cookbooks, there was always room for more. The field shifted constantly as eating habits and health issues changed. Fads came and went.

Ethnic, low-fat, traditional, specialties—Megan handled them all. She knew her way around a kitchen, too. She had lived with her grandmother's sister until the woman broke her hip. Great Aunt Ruth, a widow, had taught Megan to cook, and she'd never forgotten the time they spent together in the old-fashioned kitchen.

Now Megan counted the pages to make sure none were missing, including the illustrations and the table of contents. She liked to divide the book into sections, keeping each one in its own hanging file in a rolling cart next to her chair. Since she often worked for this particular publisher, she already knew their editorial staff preferred the index to be set up in a modified uppercase style where the actual recipe titles were capitalized, but the rest of the entries were not. There were several other ways to format an index, but Megan felt that this one was the most convenient for readers. Fortunately America's Kitchens agreed.

When she was done scanning the text, Megan set the pages aside and stood up. She rotated her shoulders and did a series of stretches, including her neck. Then she went downstairs for a glass of water. Moving around was important, especially in her condition. When she sat back down and turned on her computer she didn't immediately start working. Instead she stared at the tropical fish swimming across the screen saver as she absently reached for another piece of candy.

Mac had kissed her cheek last night, and for one precious moment she had felt like a desirable woman. It was something she'd missed, but that didn't mean he was going to slip past her defenses and complicate her life. His girlfriend probably wouldn't like that too much, either.

What kind of woman attracted a man like Mac? Megan wished she'd asked him more about Justine. From the way he had talked, either he wasn't sure how he felt about Justine or he didn't think his feelings were any of Megan's business. Of course he was right—they weren't.

With a shrug, she opened the special indexing program she used for her work. She supposed he'd be at the class tomorrow night. Meanwhile she had a living to earn.

Watching Justine walk back to the table from the ladies' room, Mac wished they'd stayed in Buttonwood instead of coming to Durango for dinner. The longer drive home was going to be decidedly awkward.

With a guilty start he realized she had made a special effort to look nice this evening and he hadn't said a thing. He hadn't missed the stares they got when they walked into the Mexican restaurant, and he'd known they weren't for him. She'd puffed up her short golden hair and she wore a blue dress that showed off her legs and her breasts.

Male heads turned as she crossed the room and returned to their table, but she didn't seem to notice. Instead she smiled at Mac as he got to his feet. Her red lips looked soft enough to sink into and she was wearing the perfume he liked.

He held out her chair and she sat down without speaking. She had seemed a little quiet during dinner, but he'd been in no hurry to begin the talk he knew they needed to have. Although she was usually undemanding, perhaps she'd gotten miffed at his failure to call as soon as he got back from Atlanta.

She was a beautiful woman, they got along well and he'd been thinking about proposing for several weeks. Was he about to make a mistake?

"Want dessert?" he asked when they were once again seated across from each other.

"Not unless you'd like to split something." She leaned back and patted her flat stomach. "You know how the camera adds pounds."

"I'd rather have a brandy," he admitted, nerves jangling.

"Then I'll keep you company with a cup of coffee." If she sensed the tension humming through him, she gave no sign.

When the waiter came to clear their plates, Mac gave him their order. While they waited, he drummed his fingers on the table and wondered what Megan was doing. Did she have friends, hobbies? He still didn't know much about her.

"Honey," Justine said, breaking into his thoughts, "why don't you tell me what's been on your mind all evening?"

Before he could answer, the waiter brought their beverages. As soon as he left again, Mac took a fortifying sip of his brandy and leaned forward, heart thudding in his chest.

"I think we should stop seeing each other," he said quietly.

Chapter Four

Except for a slight widening of her blue eyes, Justine didn't appear surprised at Mac's blunt announcement. Without looking away, she took a sip of her coffee.

"Ending our relationship is probably a good idea," she said calmly as she set her cup back down with a steady hand.

Mac had hoped she wouldn't cry or make a scene, but she was taking this awfully well. For some reason that irked him.

"Why do you say that?" he found himself asking as relief was replaced by annoyance. Didn't he mean *anything* to her? Was he just a handy escort with sleep-over privileges?

Justine reached across the table to pat his hand, irritating him further. "We both know there's been something missing from our relationship all along. I think we've gotten to be a habit with each other, and habits aren't always good."

He nearly protested that he'd been thinking about proposing to her, but he stopped himself just in time. The possibility of a future with Justine had disappeared when he'd found out he was going to be a father.

"I'm glad you understand," he said gruffly, taking a long swig of his brandy. It burned a path down his throat, making his eyes water. This wasn't going at all the way he'd planned.

"Actually, you're doing me a favor," she continued, looking way too cheerful for someone who'd just been dumped. "I've had a job offer in San Diego and I was debating whether I should take it." Absently she toyed with one of the tasteful gold earrings Mac had given her for her birthday. "Now I think you've just made that decision a lot easier."

Justine's smile trembled at the edges and her eyes glistened. Mac felt like a heel for hurting her. It was selfish to want proof that he mattered after he'd realized she didn't mean enough for him to continue their affair. What a jerk!

Guilt had him babbling. "San Diego. That's wonderful," he gushed. "It's a big promotion, isn't it? They've got a great zoo. You'll love it." He stumbled to a halt as her smile widened.

"The offer is definitely a step up to a larger market, and of course the pay's better.'' She glanced at her coffee. When she lifted her head, there was an edge of sadness to her expression, but in an instant it was gone, leaving him to wonder if he'd only imagined it. ''I'll miss you,'' she said softly. ''It's been fun.''

''Yes, it has.'' He owed her that much honesty. Justine was a warm, generous woman who had treated him well. They'd had some great times together and she'd made him happy. He wanted to tell her that, but before he could, she picked up her purse.

''I'd like to go now,'' she said.

During the drive back to Buttonwood, music from the radio helped to fill the silence that neither of them attempted to break. Night surrounded them and a light rain had started to fall. While the windshield wipers swished back and forth, Mac wondered what Justine was thinking, but he didn't ask. He was too relieved at avoiding a messy breakup to chance opening a can of worms now.

Was he making a big mistake in letting her go? They had always gotten along well, in and out of bed. She was sexy and funny. He genuinely liked her. Some marriages were based on less. As far as he was concerned, all the hype about fireworks and undying love was vastly overrated anyway. His parents had certainly gotten along fine without a lot of sappy romantic gestures and embarrassing displays of emotion.

So what was Mac's problem? Despite what Justine had told him at the restaurant, he suspected he might still be able to persuade her to stay in town if he really tried—and certainly if he proposed. She was thirty-four, although she looked younger, and she'd always insisted that once she got married her family would come ahead of her career.

Mac knew that asking her to pass up this promotion would be unfair as long as his own feelings were so confused. This was not the time to make a commitment to anyone, except of course to the child Megan carried. A clean break with Justine was the best thing for her as well as for him.

When he pulled up in front of her apartment, she finally turned to look at him. In the glow from the overhead light, he was reminded once again of the beauty that had first attracted him, but for once it failed to stir a shred of desire. Perhaps his recent trip to Atlanta had been more exhausting that he'd realized, or maybe his libido understood that this particular door was now closed.

"Don't get out," she told him as the rain drummed harder. "No point in both of us getting wet, and I can find my way."

"How soon will you be leaving?" he asked. For several months she'd held an important place in his life. He'd miss her, but not enough to change his mind, he realized belatedly.

"Now that I've come to a decision, I'll be leaving as soon as I can get everything organized. They want to fill the slot quickly, but of course I'll have to give notice at my old job. They won't have any trouble replacing me."

Mac nodded, not sure what to say.

"Tell me something," Justine asked. "What motivated you to bring this up now? Another woman?" Her voice was light, almost teasing, but her smile was brittle.

He was tempted to take the easy way out and let her think she had guessed correctly, but he owed her the truth. As briefly as he could, he told her about the baby and its mother. Her eyes widened with surprise, but she listened without interrupting.

"And Megan?" she asked when he finally wound down. "How do you feel about her?"

The question surprised him. He shrugged impatiently. "I haven't formed an opinion. She's been pretty standoffish so far, and suspicious as hell, but I'm hoping she'll come around to letting me be a part of the baby's life without having to go to court over it."

"You'd do that?" There was genuine shock in Justine's voice.

"Damn right." He didn't even have to think about it. He wasn't normally a combative person, but he'd do what he had to. "She's not raising a child of mine by herself. A kid deserves two parents."

Justine leaned over and gave him a kiss on the cheek. "I'll call you before I leave." She opened the passenger door. "Good luck with your baby, and with his mom. I hope they can give you what you're looking for.'' Before Mac could react, she'd slipped out of the pickup and hurried away, her high heels tapping on the wet pavement.

What the hell had she meant by that parting shot? Had she misunderstood what he'd said? He hadn't asked to be the father to Megan's baby, but now that he was aware it existed, he had no intentions of walking away from his responsibility to do the right thing. It was that simple.

Over the last couple of days since the first childbirth class, Megan had managed to convince herself that Mac Duncan wasn't really as attractive as she remembered. Now as she watched him studying the birthing room they'd been touring with the rest of the group, she had to admit she'd been wrong. Her mind hadn't embroidered his image, as she'd hoped.

If anything, as she gazed at his profile she found him more handsome than ever. Perhaps she'd better ask her obstetrician, Dr. Gould, if this intense physical attraction was normal at her late stage of pregnancy. Meanwhile, she'd have to be darned careful not to let him catch her staring and drooling.

''Are you all right?''

Megan blinked, vaguely aware he'd turned to ask her a question. ''I'm sorry,'' she stalled. ''I was, uh, contemplating baby names.''

Wrong thing to say. Instantly his interest intensified.

''What have you come up with?'' he asked.

Megan's mind went blank. "Nothing I'm wild about," she stammered, avoiding his gaze.

Claire, who was explaining what would happen once each of them was settled into the labor and delivery room, glanced at the two of them. "A midwife or specially trained nurse will stay with you at all times," she said.

"Maybe we can put our heads together later," Mac whispered to Megan, leaning closer. As she drank in his clean male scent, she could see the faint lines etched into the skin around his mouth and eyes. At that point, she would have agreed to just about anything.

"Sure, why not?"

"After class?" he pressed. "Dairy Freeze?"

Claire glanced at them again with a slight frown. "Does anyone have a question about the accommodations?" she asked.

Embarrassed, Megan shook her head. Claire led the way back out the door to the adjoining area where family members who weren't actually involved with the delivery could wait in comfort. The clinic was fairly new and no corners had been cut in the decoration of these maternity areas.

Since Megan hadn't told any of her relatives except one cousin that she was expecting, the roomy facility didn't really interest her. The only other family she would have liked to know about the baby, her great aunt, had died right after Megan moved to Buttonwood. She certainly didn't want the rest of them here, watching television and arguing among themselves while she delivered another child for them to resent and ignore. The thought made her shudder.

"Well?" Mac asked again. "How about it? Ice cream? Fudge sauce? It worked last time."

For once his grin irritated her. Years ago she'd outgrown the need to please anyone other than herself. She was her own person now, and she refused to be manipulated.

"I don't think so," she said coolly as they trooped back down the hallway toward their classroom. Claire had given them a short break before they resumed the session. "There's some work I need to finish when I get home."

If he was disappointed, he didn't show it. "Maybe next time," he said as he hesitated near the line to the ladies' rest room. "Is anything wrong?"

"What do you mean?" Megan asked.

He shrugged, looking sheepish, and lowered his voice. "You looked sad back there. Perhaps I could help."

She was immediately ashamed of her churlishness. It wasn't Mac's fault that she'd had an unfortunate childhood and she had no business taking her mood out on him.

"Would you like to come to lunch this weekend?" she blurted before she could reconsider. "You can see what I've done with the nursery."

His eyes widened with obvious surprise.

"I mean, if you have the time," she added, feeling foolish. "I certainly don't want to intrude on whatever plans you've made with your girlfriend." Her cheeks burned as he continued to stare. Was he frowning because he was trying to come up with a polite way to turn down her invitation?

"Justine and I broke up last night," he said just as the line moved, making room for Megan to go through the door.

She wanted to question him, but she didn't dare miss her turn in the restroom, not with another forty-five minutes of class to get through.

"I'm sorry to hear that," she said over her shoulder before the door swung shut behind her and cut off her view of Mac.

"Your boyfriend's cute," volunteered the girl Megan hadn't thought was old enough to have a baby. Her mother was taking the class with her. "I mean, for an older guy."

"Thanks," Megan replied, not bothering to correct her mistaken impression. She had to agree with the girl, whose name was Clarisse, so what was Megan's problem?

Before Clarisse could say anything further, one of the stall doors opened. By the time Megan had taken her turn, the younger girl had gone back to class. After Megan had washed her hands, freshened her lip gloss and frowned at her limp hair, she was surprised to find Mac still waiting in the hall.

"When did you want me to come to lunch?" he asked as they joined the others and Claire had once again closed the door.

There was no time to ask about his girlfriend. Now Megan wished she hadn't turned down his invitation for ice cream. She was inordinately curious about the breakup. If she hadn't been so stubborn, she could have questioned him over a strawberry sundae.

"How about Saturday?" she asked instead. "Around noon?"

He nodded. "Perfect. Don't forget to give me your address before we leave here."

Saturday dawned bright and clear. By eleven Megan could feel the warmth from the sun outside. She'd dressed in loose white pants and a simple light green top she felt emphasized her hazel eyes. She'd thought about fiddling with her hair, but finally decided to leave it straight. After all, *she* wasn't the reason Mac was coming to lunch.

The baby did a slow roll in her womb, bringing a grin to her lips. "Soon," she told the mound of her stomach as she caressed it. "Less than a month and we'll finally meet." She could hardly wait.

Meanwhile, she had a tuna salad chilling in the refrigerator, crusty cheese bread ready to pop under the broiler, iced herb tea and beer to drink. For dessert there were frosted brownies from the bakery. As much as Megan enjoyed cooking and baking, she'd found that being on her feet for too long was getting more uncomfortable as her pregnancy progressed.

Nervously she clasped her hands together and did

a quick check of the downstairs area. Earlier she had tidied her office, made her bed and glanced at the nursery, assuming that Mac might like to see where the baby would be sleeping after she brought him home. She'd scooped Cassius's litter box and swept up the trail of sand he always managed to track out of the laundry room into the downstairs hall.

A vase of pale-peach tulips and matching place mats adorned the dining room table. A scented candle burned on the kitchen counter.

Would he think she'd gone to too much trouble? She didn't want him getting the wrong idea, that she was trying to impress him. If she could have taken back the invitation after she'd blurted it out, she would have done so in a moment.

In for a penny, in for a pound, she quoted silently as she plumped up one of the pillows she'd cross-stitched for the couch. The living room was decorated in aqua, peach and tan. The carpet was beige, and white blinds covered the windows. The tiled fireplace was gas and a copper wall sculpture of soaring birds hung above the mantel. The wood furniture was whitewashed oak that matched the kitchen cabinets.

Piece by piece, Megan had created a home here, and now she was creating a family, two things she'd never had before. Two things she'd planned on doing without interference from anyone else.

The doorbell rang, sending Cassius slinking up the staircase to the safety beneath her bed. He might look like a show cat, but in reality he was a stray she'd rescued from a shelter. Beneath his haughty facade he was as wary of strangers as Megan was herself.

Hoping this wasn't a big mistake, she plastered on a welcoming smile and opened the door. Sunglasses screened Mac's expression. He was holding a brightly colored bouquet. Tucked under his other arm was a brown stuffed bunny.

"I hope I'm not too early," he said, offering the flowers to Megan.

"No, of course not. Come on in." She thanked him for the blooms—yellow daffodils, red and white tulips and sprigs of greenery—as she opened the door wider and moved aside.

Tucking his sunglasses into his shirt pocket, he stopped in the entry and looked around with obvious interest.

"This is really nice."

They were having a baby together and acting like strangers. Suddenly Megan was fed up with the stilted politeness between them. "I'm sure it's not what you're used to, but it's fine for me," she said defensively.

He arched his brow as she bit her lip in embarrassment at her own rudeness. "You think I live in one of my playhouses?" he asked, deliberately misunderstanding her as she led the way through the living room.

Megan got a vase from the china cabinet and filled it with water from the kitchen sink. Before she turned around, she took a deep breath. "I just figured you for a home owner," she explained. "I can't picture someone with his own business living in an apartment." Even though Mac was dressed casually in faded jeans and a striped polo shirt, he probably had one of those big places with a three-car garage in the ritzy development outside of town.

"Yes," he admitted, "I have a house I'm rather proud of. You'll have to come by sometime."

Megan bobbed her head. "Sure thing." She had driven through Eastridge a couple of times, and now she pictured Mac standing in front of a fancy brick showplace with soaring windows and a multi-level tile roof, surrounded by sterile, professionally landscaped grounds. He probably had a pool in the back and an elaborate wrought-iron gate across the sweeping driveway to keep out the riffraff.

She finished arranging the flowers he'd brought and set them on the bar that divided the kitchen from the dining room. Although the intense colors clashed with her pastel decor and the peach tulips on the table, they brought spring inside in a vibrant way.

"This is for the baby. I didn't know what you'd already have." He set the plush bunny on the counter, where it promptly fell over onto its side.

Megan had a weakness for stuffed animals and kept several on her bed. Automatically she set the bunny upright, her fingers lingering in its soft fur. "It's adorable. I'm sure he'll love it." Had anyone ever dealt with a situation quite this bizarre before?

"Would you like a beer or some iced tea?" she asked. What did he really think about her place? That it was too small to raise a child? Too fussy? That the stairs weren't safe? She'd planned on getting a baby gate when the time came.

Mac had gone to stand in front of her china cabinets, hands jammed into his pockets as he studied the collection of old salt-and-pepper shakers she'd inherited from Aunt Ruth. They were all Megan had left of the one family member who had made her feel wanted. She was prepared for a comment about the tacky little figures, but Mac didn't make one.

"Iced tea sounds fine," he said instead. "Thank you again for inviting me over."

As Megan recalled how many times she'd picked up the phone to cancel, her cheeks burned with guilt. "I thought you'd like to see where the baby would be sleeping," she explained as she poured their tea, adding lemon wedges and long-handled spoons.

Mac turned to her and his expression brightened. "Yeah, I'd love that." He accepted the glass she handed him and lifted it slightly. "To our partnership," he said with a wry grin. He must find this whole business as awkward as she did.

Startled by his gesture, Megan let him touch the rim of his glass lightly to hers. This was really getting out of hand.

He took a long swallow of the tea, the muscles of his tanned throat rippling, then he set down his glass and leaned against the counter.

"Do you have everything you need for the baby?" he asked. "A crib, enough diapers, whatever the well-outfitted infant requires these days?"

Megan had to struggle with the instant defensiveness that shot up like a protective wall. No doubt he meant well. "Yes, except for a few odds and ends, I think I have what I need."

"Clothing?" he persisted. "Babies seem to grow pretty fast. Bottles?"

"I plan to nurse," she said without thinking. "It's healthier."

His glance dropped to her breasts and Megan nearly raised her hands to cover herself. It wasn't as though he were ogling her. Somehow the realization that he was merely assessing her equipment was more annoying than if he had been.

"I'd like to help," he said hesitantly. "Financially, I mean."

She froze. "What did you have in mind?"

He scratched his chin while he considered. "The kid's mine, too. I should share in some of the responsibility—"

He broke off abruptly as Megan started shaking her head. "No, no, no. That's not necessary. I don't need your help."

Mac took a step closer and suddenly the kitchen seemed cramped. "Then what do you want from me?" he asked, frustration easy to see on his rugged face.

"Nothing!" Megan cried, backing up until she

bumped into the counter behind her. "Getting involved was your idea, not mine."

Mac swung away as if she'd slapped him. "You won't give me a chance," he accused as he stared out the window, shoulders hunched.

Instantly Megan felt ashamed of her selfishness. Nothing could change the fact that he was the father of her child. If she didn't make room for him voluntarily, there was a good chance he might force her to do so legally.

Moving closer, she touched his arm. The muscle stiffened beneath her hand as he stared down at her, dark eyes brimming with frustration.

"I'm at a real loss here," he said harshly.

"I'm sorry." She struggled to explain her feelings. "I guess I've been thinking about having this baby alone for so long that it's hard now to let anyone else in. I need time to adjust. Can you understand?"

He stared at her until she thought he might slam out of her house. Then his tense expression relaxed just a little. Hands on hips, he stared at the floor.

"Yeah," he said, breaking the silence that had grown as fragile as a spun-sugar sculpture. "I guess I've been pushing you pretty hard."

His generosity astounded her. It was Megan's turn to stare. "Thank you," she whispered. "It's nice of you to share the blame."

"If you'd rather, we could blame your hormones," he suggested outrageously. When she gaped, he looked embarrassed. "I bought a book about having kids and I've just finished the chapter on mood swings and stuff. It must be hard to not always be in control, a little like riding a roller coaster.''

She couldn't help but grin at his discomfiture. The idea of him reading up on the subject was rather sweet.

''Sometimes it's difficult,'' she admitted. ''But being prepared helps a lot. So far a sudden obsession for chocolate has been one of the most obvious changes I've noticed about myself.''

His stance relaxed visibly. ''Yeah, I saw the bowl of M&M's in the living room.''

''I have them stashed all over the house,'' she confessed. For a moment they stood smiling at each other like idiots. Then Mac shifted and cleared his throat. Megan grabbed her iced tea and took a long drink. The awkward moment passed.

''Would you like to see the nursery before we eat?'' she asked. Maybe he didn't give a darn what it looked like, but she was proud of the way the wallpaper and curtains had turned out.

''In a minute,'' he said as she turned to lead him up the stairs. ''There's something else I'd like to do first.''

She glanced back around and a shiver of warning slid down her spine at the intensity on his face. ''What?''

He rubbed a finger along one sideburn and glanced down at his feet. She noticed that he had on well-worn cowboy boots and she wondered distractedly if he had horses. That would account for his tan. There was still so much she didn't know.

"Is the baby moving?" he asked, surprising her yet again. What had she expected, that he was about to make a pass? She was hardly in the condition to push his buttons on *that* level.

"You mean right now?" she squeaked, one hand splaying protectively on her abdomen.

His gaze followed the movement with naked hunger. At last she understood. Moving closer, she took his hand in hers. Goodness, but she could feel the strength there.

Gaze locked on his dark one, she pressed his palm to her stomach. As she did so, the baby let out a kick worthy of a karate black belt. Mac snatched back his hand as though he'd been burned. A look of wonder crossed his face. As Megan stood motionless, he reached out tentatively, his eyes asking permission. Scarcely daring to breathe, she nodded.

Gently, slowly, he touched her again. They waited in silence, but the baby refused to move. As Mac loomed over her, the spot where his hand rested seemed to grow warmer. The toasty heat spread through her, followed by a feeling of incredible peace. Was she the only one to feel the bond between them, she wondered.

The baby poked again, just under Mac's hand. A huge grin spread over his face. "Was that his foot?" he asked as he let her go with obvious reluctance.

Megan shrugged, smiling back at him as tears threatened. "A heel or maybe an elbow," she guessed.

Mac must have seen the glimmer of moisture in her eyes. He peered closer. "Are you okay? Did I hurt you?"

"Oh, no." She struggled for an explanation. How could she tell him that this was the first time she'd had someone to share, really share, in her excitement?

"Hormones," she said instead, with a damp chuckle. "That's all."

He didn't appear convinced. "If you say so. Do you need to sit down, or are you able to climb the stairs? I'd still like to see the baby's room, if that's okay."

Great. Now he thought she was some fragile flower who was too weak to take care of herself. "I'm fine. Let's go." Irritated with both herself and, unaccountably, him as well, she led the way to the nursery.

Chapter Five

As Mac followed Megan up the stairs of her town house he noticed that, except for the careful way she moved, he wouldn't have suspected from this angle that she was pregnant. Below the blouse that covered her bottom, her loose white pants disguised the shape of her legs and sparked his curiosity until he remembered that he was interested in her only as a mother.

"My office is through there," she said with a wave of her hand before she went down the hall-way.

Mac would have liked to check out where she worked. "How did you get started indexing books?"

''Long story,'' she said over her shoulder as they walked past her bedroom.

Mac glimpsed a feminine environment through the partially closed door, a splash of flowers and several teddy bears on the bed, sunlight filtering through pale, sheer curtains.

''I've always liked to cook, and I met a woman who indexes history texts,'' she continued, stopping in an open doorway at the end of the hall. ''Her publisher was looking for someone to do a series of cookbooks. My friend didn't have time, so she showed me the basics. I took a course and the rest was history.''

The room they were in was small, but it was bright and cheerful. Quite a bit of care and planning had gone into it.

''In case the crib didn't clue you in, this is the nursery,'' Megan said as he looked around.

''Did you decorate it yourself?'' he asked as he bent down to peer at a teddy bear night light. Everything in the room had been chosen with obvious care and love. He had no business feeling left out, but he did.

The window looked over a grassy central area bisected by brick walkways. In the middle was a big round planter filled with flowers and surrounded by benches.

''The curtains were easy to sew, but this was my first attempt at wallpapering.'' Megan pointed at the border that circled the room. ''I think it turned out pretty well.''

A row of animal faces smiled down at Mac. "You did a good job." He thought of the layers of paper he'd removed from the dining room walls at his house before he got down to bare plaster. If he had known Megan earlier, he could have helped her with this room. He wondered whether she would have let him. "It's a nice complex. I'm sure our baby will be very happy here."

A fierce swell of emotion surged into his throat and he had to swallow hard. Would he ever be used to the idea of his child being raised by someone else? Right now he doubted it.

Luckily Megan had been straightening a picture on the wall and hadn't noticed his lapse. "If you've seen enough, let's go down and eat lunch," she suggested, heading for the hall.

Mac was a little disappointed that she didn't offer to show him the rest of the upstairs, but he wasn't about to ask. He'd already figured out that she guarded her privacy and he didn't want to push. Another quick glimpse was all he saw of her bedroom and her office on his way by. He didn't want to get caught snooping. He was still bemused that she had invited him over. Maybe there was hope for them after all.

"Can I help?" he offered when they got back to the kitchen. It was spotlessly clean and the light colors made it seem more spacious than it actually was. The dining room table, he'd noticed earlier, was set for two.

"Everything's ready except the bread," she re-

plied. "You can get the salad out of the fridge."
She slid a pan into the oven. "I hope you like
tuna."

"As a matter of fact, I do." Sliced egg, tomato
wedges, olives, carrot curls, and a mound of tuna
mixture were all arranged on a bed of shredded let-
tuce in a large bowl. "This looks great." Mac realized he was famished. "Do you want it on the
table?"

"Yes, that's fine. The bread will only take a couple of minutes." Megan refilled both their glasses
while Mac watched her, hands in his pockets. Despite her extra weight, she moved easily around the
kitchen and he found himself speculating about her
shape beneath her loose clothing.

By the time she'd brought out a bowl of creamy
salad dressing and a plate of brownies, the cheese
bread was browned and bubbly. As she set the hot
plate down on a colorful trivet, Mac pulled out one
of the chairs for her.

"Thank you." She looked surprised by the gesture.

Once she was settled, he sat down across from
her and spread his napkin, peach plaid like the place
mats, on his lap.

"Thank my mother," he replied. "She taught me
all I know."

"I'll be sure to, if I see her." Megan passed him
the salad and helped herself to a slice of the hot
cheese bread.

"You can be sure that you will." He selected a

pickle from a pretty oval dish. "She and my father will both want to meet you."

"Have you told them?" she asked. "About the baby?"

"Not yet." Mac dug into the salad. He hadn't figured out how he was going to explain the situation to them. He was tempted to ask Megan to pretend they had a relationship, but he immediately discarded the idea. A long-range deception of that magnitude was bound to turn into a nightmare.

"What about your parents?" he asked when they had both filled their plates. "Are they excited?" How did they feel about their daughter becoming a single parent?

Megan sipped her tea, eyes downcast. "They were killed in a car accident when I was five."

"Good Lord, that's awful. I'm so sorry." Mac felt clumsy. He didn't know what else to say.

"It was a long time ago." Her voice was sad for a moment, but then she lifted her chin. "I've adjusted."

He wondered how a person got used to something that traumatic. "You were so little. Who raised you after they died?"

A shutter came down over her face and she began to pick at her salad. "I went to stay with a great aunt." She glanced at the china cabinet and Mac recalled the silly little figures displayed there. "She broke her hip when I was seven and went into a nursing home. After that I moved around a lot."

"Foster care?" Mac had heard the stories. No

doubt many foster parents were kind, but not all. Would the adversity in Megan's childhood affect her parenting ability? He might yet have to seek legal advice if he suspected that there were problems.

The last thing Megan wanted was pity, especially from Mac Duncan. "I was raised by various relatives." Spearing a tomato wedge, she wished they'd never started on this subject. It wasn't a time in her life that she enjoyed reflecting on.

"Were you happy?" he probed.

She didn't want to answer, but neither did she care to appear rude. Although she would have preferred to sidestep his question with a generic remark, she figured he deserved the truth.

"They had families of their own," she explained. "No one really had room for me, so I'd stay for a few months and then it would be someone else's turn." She had grown up feeling as though she didn't belong anywhere.

Frowning, Mac set down his fork. "That must have been very hard for you, especially when you were still grieving for your parents. You had no siblings?"

"No." Just cousins who seemed to resent her presence, she remembered with a jumble of emotions. "What about you?" She pictured him as part of an extended family, roughhousing with his brothers and teasing his sisters.

He chewed and swallowed a bite of cheese bread. "This is delicious."

Megan acknowledged the compliment impatiently. She was glad he liked the food, but she was more interested in learning about him. The more time they spent together, the more drawn to him she was. At some point she'd have to put on the brakes, but not just yet.

"I'm an only child, too." His answer surprised her. "My parents are both college professors at Denver U. Dad's the head of the physics department and Mother's specialty is English Lit."

Megan was surprised. He didn't strike her as having come from that kind of exalted background. "So the description the clinic gave me about you was accurate," she quipped, popping an olive into her mouth.

Mac frowned, and then suddenly his expression cleared. "Our kid ain't getting no weak genes from my side of the family tree," he drawled with an outrageous wink.

His clowning made her chuckle, his easy grin churning up a more than matronly response in her. If he had the slightest clue to the lustful thoughts of a woman who walked with a waddle and could barely reach her toes, he'd be grossed out for sure.

"Your parents must have doted on you," she said to distract them both.

Mac set down his fork, his expression suddenly somber. "I wouldn't exactly say that." Instead of elaborating, he took a long swallow of his iced tea.

How hard could his childhood have been, with two parents who had interesting and respectable careers? They probably weren't rich, but he would have had the benefits of a stable, upper-class environment. Megan would have liked to ask more about it, but then she remembered that there was something else she wanted to know even more.

The other evening he'd mentioned breaking up with his girlfriend. Surely he wouldn't have mentioned the subject if he intended it to be off-limits.

"So," she asked around a mouthful of tuna salad. "What happened with Justine?"

Mac toyed with his silverware and she thought he was going to ignore her question. Then he looked up, dark eyes unreadable, and shrugged. "She was offered a promotion in California. Turning it down would have been a bad career move."

"What does she do?" Megan asked. Something more exciting than indexing cookbooks, she'd bet.

"She's a news anchor at KORO, the local cable TV station."

"Of course, Justine Connors," Megan exclaimed, dismayed. "I've seen her. She's very attractive." The woman had a sophisticated style Megan could never compete with, especially not in her present condition.

Compete? Where had that idea come from?

"So she was the one who ended it?" Megan probed. "I'm sorry." She was dying to ask whether his heart was broken. If it was, he hid it well.

Not long ago Megan had wanted him to be involved with someone else, hoping he wouldn't make changes in his life on account of the baby, and now she was almost jealous of his possible feelings for another woman. It was getting more difficult to keep her emotional distance from Mac. She'd better remember that he must regard her as little more than a human incubator, or she'd be the one with a broken heart.

"I guess you could say our decision to end our relationship was mutual." His expression was philosophical. "Things change."

Was he hiding his pain behind a macho facade, or did he really not give a fig? It was impossible to tell for sure, and she sure as heck wasn't going to pry any further or he'd wonder why she found his love life so interesting.

Mac had finished his salad and now he reached for a brownie. "May I? These look good." His brow quirked attractively.

Megan was surprised to realize that she, too, had cleaned her plate while they were talking. As they finished up with a chocolate boost, their conversation turned more general, as though they had silently agreed they'd done enough mutual probing for one day.

She got up to refill Mac's glass and he polished off two more brownies as their conversation drifted from movies they'd seen to the music they liked and then to local politics. Mac believed the city council's desire to pass more zoning laws was stifling, while Megan believed controlled growth was vitally important to the community.

"I shouldn't have to get permission to cut down

a tree on my own property,'' Mac argued. ''If there's a danger some brittle old cottonwood is going to drop a branch through my roof, I have the right to deal with it. I'm sure not going to go berserk and take out a stand of aspen with a chain saw for no reason.''

''Not everyone feels the same way you do,'' Megan insisted. ''Just last year a developer did exactly that. Two streets over from here the sidewalk was lined with a row of lovely old birch trees. Before anyone knew what was going on, they were butchered to widen the parking lot.''

Mac frowned. ''I remember those trees. One day when I drove by, they were lying on the ground in pieces. I wondered what had happened.'' He set aside his plate. ''Just because one idiot acted irresponsibly still doesn't mean we need more regulations, though. Too many laws and you can't get anything done.''

Megan could see there was no point in arguing. At least they had a few common interests. They both liked country music, comedies and hiking. He seemed quite interested in hearing about the mining towns she'd explored and he asked several questions. She was actually surprised that, given his background, Mac's tastes weren't more cultured. He liked baseball, but admitted that ballet and the opera bored him to tears.

And she'd been right about one thing. He was an expert skier.

''I don't go as often as I'd like,'' he admitted.

"And I travel on business way too often, but that will change as Small World's reputation grows."

Megan wanted to ask him about his company, but she figured he might not have intended to stay all afternoon. She glanced at the wall clock in the kitchen, surprised to see how much time had gone by.

Mac must have followed the direction of her gaze, because he immediately slid back his chair. "I'd better be going," he said as he rose and started stacking his dirty dishes. "Let me help you to clean up first."

"That's not necessary," Megan protested, trying to take his plate out of his hands. "You're company."

"And you're pregnant," he replied. "Why don't you go put your feet up. I can figure out where things go."

"I'm not an invalid," she scolded, grabbing her own dishes and silver before he could get to them. His willingness to help deserved a mark in the plus column, though. So many men wouldn't be caught dead in a kitchen unless it was to get another cold one from the refrigerator. None of the men in the families she'd stayed with growing up had helped with the housework, even though one of her aunts had worked full-time and another relative had two small children of her own.

At least Megan had known going into this situation that she would be doing all the work connected with raising a child, not like some new mothers who expected help and never got it.

By the time they'd cleared away the food, loaded the dishwasher and wiped off the counters, working companionably in the small kitchen, Megan's back was starting to nag and she had to suppress more than one yawn. She hadn't been sleeping well and sometimes took a nap in the afternoon.

"Thanks again for lunch," Mac said as she walked him to the door. "I like your place."

"Thank you for the flowers and the bunny." She'd enjoyed his company more than she'd expected she would. It was obvious that he was trying hard to get along.

He stood looking down at her. "You're an easy person to be with," he said, surprising her. Before she could think of a reply, he leaned forward and kissed her gently on the cheek.

The touch of his lips sparked a yearning that caught Megan by surprise. Without thinking, she swayed toward him. He started to straighten and then he hesitated. Warmth flowed through her as his gaze dropped to her mouth. Did he think she was begging for another kiss?

She wanted to pull away, but he cupped her chin in his big, rough hand. He dipped his head as if he, too, was drawn by an invisible force, and touched his lips to hers.

Her breath caught and her lips parted. He broke the tentative contact.

His gaze, dark as melted chocolate, probed hers.

She was barely aware of her hands lifting to his chest, her fingers clutching his shirt. With a groan he wrapped his arms around her, pulling her closer. His mouth covered hers again, more insistently, more commandingly. For an instant she yielded to the sweet pressure and felt the touch of his tongue.

Reaction exploded inside her.

He lifted his mouth, changed the angle of the kiss and deepened it. Megan crowded closer, her swollen stomach pressed against his arousal. Lips and tongues meshed, tasted, caressed. Her breasts were on fire. His hands slid to her hips, his fingers biting into her soft flesh.

Mac let her go so abruptly that she nearly stumbled. He grabbed her arms and steadied her, his touch subtly different from a moment before.

"You okay?" His voice was gratifyingly husky.

Megan blinked twice, rapidly. What had happened here? Mac looked as stunned as she felt. He was already reaching for the door knob.

"I'll see you at class," he said and then he was gone.

Megan's first hysterical thought was thank goodness she hadn't turned the dead bolt as she often did when she was home or he might have thought she was locking him in with her. Laughter bubbled up and threatened to spill through her still tingling lips. Hysterical laughter. Her second thought was to sit down before her knees crumpled.

From outside she heard an engine start and assumed it was Mac, making his escape from the crazy pregnant woman.

The image wiped away the last traces of amusement. She sank onto the couch and buried her face in her hands. How could she have acted the way she did? So desperate, so needy?

Cassius must have decided it was safe enough to come out from beneath her bed and pad silently down the stairs. Now he butted her leg and meowed.

Megan lifted her head. "Some help you were," she told him as he stared up at her, eyes as round as gold coins. She scooped him into her arms. "Couldn't you have bitten me on the ankle and stopped me from making a fool of myself?"

The tone of her voice must have upset him. When he started to squirm, she let him go.

Obviously unimpressed by her human problems, the cat wandered through the pet door to the closet containing his litter box and dishes. His ID tag clinked against the edge of his empty bowl in wordless reproach.

"You men are all alike—" Megan called out, "only thinking of yourselves." Even as she said the words, she knew that in Mac's case they weren't true. All *he* was interested in was the baby she carried.

How depressing.

Mac thought about that kiss for two days. On Monday morning as he sat in his office and looked out the window instead of drawing the plans for a new log cabin playhouse, he was still trying to sort out what had happened.

One moment he'd been giving Megan a platonic thank-you peck on the cheek for a nice time and the next they'd been plastered together like tarpaper on plywood. He still wasn't sure how the situation had gone so wrong so fast. All Mac knew was that he wanted to see her again and find out if the kiss had been a moment straight out of the twilight zone or the start of something he had no business getting into.

If he was the kind of man who bought into the romantic hype of happily ever after he might think falling for Megan was the answer to his problems. Too bad he wasn't that naive. He knew a marketing pitch when he stepped in one. Sure, he'd considered marrying Justine at one point, but they would both have gone into it with eyes wide open. No unreasonable expectations, no disappointment and no hurt feelings.

It had taken a broken relationship and subsequent bruised heart some years ago before the lesson he should have learned from his own parents finally sank in. Mac wasn't usually big on analyzing his feelings, but he'd never had a child to consider before. One misstep with Megan could cost him more than he was willing to pay.

The phone rang, but Mac ignored it. A moment later his office manager, Elaine, stuck her head in the doorway.

"Call for you," she said. "Dennis Reid from the clinic."

Maybe Dennis finally had come up with some answers for Mac. Hopeful, he reached for the phone.

"Sorry I haven't gotten back to you sooner," Dennis said with a gloat in his voice. "I've been distracted by a certain senorita, if you catch my drift."

Mac knew he was expected to show interest. He jammed down his impatience. "The same woman you told me about before?" he asked. "Rachel, wasn't it?" He'd never understood men who needed to brag about their conquests. Some things should remain private.

"Yeah, Rachel Arquette," Dennis replied. "She's one hot number, a nurse here at the clinic. My mind hasn't been on my work lately."

"Considering the field you're in, that could be a problem," Mac said dryly.

Dennis laughed. "I manage."

Mac remained silent. Dennis must have realized he wasn't going to angle for details. He cleared his throat. "I still don't have any news about your situation," he admitted.

Annoyed, Mac sat up straighter. He'd been listening to Dennis's bull for nothing! "How the hell long does it take to get a few simple answers?" he exploded.

"Hey, hey, buddy," Dennis cautioned. "Take it easy. Don't shoot the messenger. I told you it's not my area of responsibility. I'm just trying to do a friend a favor here.''

Mac winced. Except for playing racquetball together, he didn't consider the other man a friend. Not only was Dennis a poor loser, his blatant attempts to cover up what Mac assumed was his basic insecurity with bragging eroded Mac's patience.

''What's the problem now?'' Mac asked without bothering to hide his irritation.

Dennis's chuckle grated on his already frayed temper. ''Apparently your file has been misplaced. Until it turns up, I can't find out a thing.''

''What about Megan Malone's file?'' Mac demanded.

''Who?''

''The recipient of my little donation,'' Mac ground out between clenched teeth. ''Is her file missing, as well?''

''No need to get sarcastic,'' Dennis replied. ''It will be tricky, her information being confidential and all, but I'll see what I can do.''

''I know all about the clinic's policy on confidentiality,'' Mac snapped. It was nearly more than he could do to thank Dennis and hang up before he burst out with a string of swear words he hadn't voiced since the last time he'd smashed his thumb with a hammer. Then he kicked the file cabinet next to his drafting table hard enough to dent the front of it and bruise his toe.

''Is this a bad time?''

Mac swung around in his chair to see Megan

standing hesitantly in the open doorway wearing a long, blue denim dress and sandals. Her hair was pinned up off her shoulders and silver hoops danced at her ears.

How much of his conversation had she heard? Damn Elaine for letting her come back here without warning him first. The heat of embarrassment swept up Mac's neck and scorched his cheeks as he shot to his feet, toe throbbing dully.

"Uh, hi," he said hoarsely. "What brings you here?"

It was Megan's turn to blush. "I wanted to bring you the booklet Claire asked that we read before class tomorrow. I forgot to give it to you on Saturday." She glanced over her shoulder. "There was no one at the desk out front and I thought I heard your voice, so I just wandered back. I should have waited."

Elaine must be taking a smoke break. Mac had forgotten all about the booklet on birthing techniques the doctor had handed out to each couple on Thursday. Megan gripped it tightly as she hovered in the doorway.

"Come on in," he invited her hastily. "I didn't mean to be so rude." He lifted a stack of files off his extra chair in silent invitation and set them on the floor. "I just had an upsetting phone call," he explained as she sat down with a sigh. Maybe she'd let slip how much she'd overheard.

"From the way you were assaulting your file cabinet when I got here, I figured it wasn't good news,'' she replied with a frown of concern. ''I hope it wasn't someone canceling an order. The pictures of your playhouses I saw in the outer office are fantastic. I'd love to see the real thing sometime.''

Mac was flattered by her interest and relieved that she apparently hadn't heard him discussing her with Dennis. ''Would you like a tour right now?'' he offered.

She shook her head with obvious regret. ''I have a doctor's appointment in a few minutes. I just came by to give you this, so you'd have time to read it before tomorrow night. I'm sorry I forgot all about it the other day.''

Mac remembered how their last meeting had ended. Obviously Megan did, too, because she stood back up and set the booklet down on his desk as though it had suddenly gotten too hot to hang on to. Even moving as awkwardly as she did, she managed to remain extremely appealing in the denim dress. What people said about pregnant women must be true. Megan's skin was glowing and her hair, looking like strands of dark-gold silk, was caught up in a silver clip that left her neck exposed and made him think about nibbling his way from her earlobe to her collarbone and back again. He had to be demented.

The memory of the kiss they'd shared seemed to hover between them like a giant balloon they were both determined to ignore no matter how obvious its presence.

"Thanks for coming by," Mac said politely. He would have offered to go to the doctor with her, but he figured she'd think he was crowding her, so he didn't mention it. "I hope your appointment goes well," he said instead. "No problems, I hope?"

"Oh, no. Dr. Gould assures me that I'm as healthy as a peasant woman." Her eyes widened, and Mac realized she'd spoken without thinking.

"I'm glad to hear it," he drawled, smiling to dispel any awkwardness. "If you do give birth in the field, you'll save some money on the hospital bill."

To his relief, Megan's serious expression dissolved into a smile. "I have to run," she said with regret in her voice. At least she didn't seem worried that he'd pounce on her again. "Can I have a rain check on the tour? I'd love to look around."

To his surprise, he realized he was reluctant to let her leave, even knowing the chance of another heated clinch if she stayed was slim at best.

"I'll go you one better," he suggested rashly. "I've seen your place. It's lovely. Why don't you come over for dinner before class tomorrow and I'll show you mine?"

"I don't know where you live," she hedged, glancing at her watch, "and I'm afraid if I don't leave right now I'll be late for my appointment."

"I'll call you with directions," Mac said quickly. "If you aren't home, I'll leave them on your machine."

Still she hesitated.

"Come on," he urged. "We both have to eat. If you come by my house at five, we'll still get to class in plenty of time."

She took a deep breath that strained the denim covering her rounded breasts. "Okay. Tomorrow at five. Bye for now."

Before he could reply, she hurried back down the hall. No sooner had the outer door shut behind her than his silver-haired office manager appeared in front of him with her hands on her ample hips.

"Who was that, a prospective customer?" she demanded. "I didn't see her come in, but she looks ready to deliver in short order. Does she want a playhouse for the new baby?"

Mac grinned, feeling suddenly light-hearted. "If you'd only quit smoking like I suggested, you would have been at your desk where you belong and you could have asked her yourself," he teased. "Now I guess you'll just have to wonder."

Chapter Six

When Megan got home from her doctor's appointment, pleased to have heard that both she and the baby were doing fine, she found a carton by the front door. It wasn't heavy, so Megan carried it inside, set it on the table and glanced at the return address.

What could her cousin be sending? Megan had gone to live with Wendy, her two brothers and her parents—Megan's aunt and uncle on her father's side—after Great Aunt Ruth fell and broke her hip. Megan had just turned eight and Wendy was eleven. After a year, Aunt Sandra had a new baby and Megan was passed on to another relative.

Except for a dutiful card each Christmas, Megan

didn't keep in touch with any of them. Wendy had written a few times over the years, but Megan's replies were brief. In a weak moment, she'd mentioned her pregnancy, regretting the impulse almost immediately afterwards.

Now she opened the box and peered inside. On top was a note.

Dear Megan,
Here are some things I thought you could use, if you don't mind hand-me-downs.
Babies grow so fast.
Let me know how you're doing.
Love,

Wendy

Megan set aside the note and lifted out two piles of neatly folded clothes—tiny sleepers in unisex prints and stripes, booties the size of her thumb, undershirts, nighties, bibs no bigger than her palm and two darling sun hats, one white and the other red with navy piping. All the clothing had been laundered many times, but none appeared badly worn.

Megan thought Wendy had two children of her own, but she wasn't positive. The last time Megan had seen any of her relatives had been at Aunt Ruth's funeral in Cheyenne, but Megan left straight from the cemetery. She preferred doing her grieving alone.

In the bottom of the box, neatly folded, was a

daffodil-yellow blanket that was obviously new. Megan took it out and laid it on the table. It was knit in a zigzag design and was as soft as the fur on a kitten's tummy. As she examined the blanket more closely, she saw a couple of mistakes in the stitching. Curious, she turned it over, looking for a tag. In one corner was a small label. Knit for you by Wendy.

Megan's fingers trembled on the yarn and her vision blurred. Other than the bunny Mac had brought over, this was her baby's first real present. She was astounded that anyone from her family would have gone to the trouble. Growing up, she'd been a nuisance, a burden, a shy child who never fit in. When she'd stayed with Aunt Sandra, Wendy had been three years older and resented sharing her room. Megan was continually surprised she bothered to stay in touch.

After Megan had refolded the blanket, she took everything upstairs. She stacked the clothing in a dresser drawer in the nursery, rearranging it twice, and draped the blanket over the crib railing.

What did Wendy, married to a pharmacist in Reno, think of Megan having a baby without a father? Without a husband, she corrected herself. She would have liked to tell Mac about the gift, but she'd interrupted his work once already today. After she wrote Wendy a thank-you note, she called a girlfriend instead. Patty wasn't home, so Megan turned on her computer and went to work on the dessert cookbook. Halfway through the chapter on pies, she got up and wandered into the nursery just to look at the blanket and Mac's bunny sitting in a corner of the crib.

When the baby stirred restlessly in her womb, she wished Mac were here so he could feel it move. She liked the way his hand felt pressed against her. There was something solid about him.

The next day went by too quickly. Being nervous about going to Mac's house was silly. It wasn't a date.

Late in the afternoon, Megan glanced at the time and saved her day's work on the computer. She'd been sitting for too long—her back ached in protest, but it would ease up once she moved around. After a quick shower, she changed into a long, loose-fitting summer dress in deference to the heat.

She thought about taking the blanket to show Mac, but changed her mind. Men weren't interested in things like that and she wasn't sure herself why Wendy's gesture meant so much to her. Like Aunt Ruth's salt-and-pepper collection, the blanket was something that could be passed on someday. Boy or girl, she would make sure her baby understood the importance of family keepsakes.

For the third time in a half hour, Mac went outside and squinted up at the cloudless blue sky while Rusty watched from beside the fountain. Thanks to a huge cottonwood, the deck Mac had built off the back of the house would still be in partial shade when it came time for dinner. Good thing he'd planned a barbecue. It was too darn warm to fire up the kitchen range.

He glanced at the patio table, set with a blue checkered cloth and an old milk can full of daisies. It was clear that Megan liked homey touches and he was determined to show her he wasn't a complete barbarian.

He checked the glowing coals and then his watch. Before he went back inside to make sure nothing had gotten messy or dusty since the last time he'd looked, the sound of a car coming down the driveway alerted him to Megan's arrival. Rusty ran to the backyard gate, barking loudly, and then he charged up the steps to the deck.

"Quiet down," Mac said impatiently. "It's okay." He hadn't thought to ask if she liked dogs, but no one minded Rusty.

With the Irish Setter at his heels, Mac walked through the house and pulled open the front door as Megan got out of the car. She was wearing a sun dress printed with orange poppies, but her expression was strained. Was she nervous about coming here?

"Everything okay?" he asked as he walked out to meet her.

Megan's expression cleared. Even three weeks away from her due date, she managed to look terrific. "I'm fine. Who's this?" She extended a hand to Rusty, standing at Mac's side.

The Irish Setter sniffed her fingers politely as Mac introduced him.

"Aren't you a pretty boy," she crooned, sneaking her fingers around to scratch the dog's ears. His tail swept back and forth like a big orange feather as Megan handed Mac a brightly colored gift-bag.

"I'm glad I didn't bring flowers." She looked at his overflowing beds. "Your yard is lovely."

"Gardening is one of my hobbies. Digging in the dirt relaxes me. Those tulips I brought you came from out back."

Megan hadn't pictured him involved in anything so mundane. She was still trying to adjust to the sight of the lovely though unpretentious old house. Even in his knit shirt and khaki shorts, gift-bag dangling from one hand, Mac looked far too successful to be doing his own yard work.

"Living in a condo, I've found that gardening is one thing I miss," she confided, trying to ignore her sizzling reaction to his gaze. "Mine is confined to a couple of containers on my patio."

The dog thrust its nose against her hand in a bid for attention and Mac smiled down at her as though her presence pleased him. For once she wasn't going to dwell on the real reason he was interested.

"I'm surprised by your house," she confessed as he led the way up the front steps.

He turned and cocked an eyebrow. "How so?"

"I expected you to live in one of those showplaces in Eastridge."

"Are you disappointed?" he asked.

"Oh, no, no! This is charming. It has character."

His house was in an old part of town, set back from the quiet road and surrounded by mature trees.

"That's exactly what I thought when I first saw it. The house and yard were run-down then and it's still a work in progress, but I always like a challenge." His white teeth flashed as he pushed the door open wider and stepped aside.

"Welcome," he said, bowing gallantly.

Blushing, Megan went past him into the entry. Although the house was beautiful, she was more aware of her host than her surroundings. She made the appropriate comments and he thanked her for the candle she'd brought, a squat vanilla cube she'd figured would blend with any decor. As he led the way to the French doors at the back of the house, she got the impression of rich colors, polished wood and lazy ceiling fans. Mostly she watched the back of his dark head and listened to his deep voice.

"Someone had painted all the wood trim dark brown," he said as she noticed the honeyed oak in the dining room.

"What a crime," Megan murmured. Tall windows let in the light. Soft peach walls added warmth.

"There's a bathroom if you need it," he added, pointing to an alcove and a partially opened door.

"I think the question is when, not if," she replied.

"If you're interested, I can show you the rest of the house after we eat," he suggested. "I thought I'd barbecue, and the coals are ready."

It was obvious to Megan that he was proud of his home, and well he should be. Granted, she hadn't noticed every detail, but what she'd seen was lovely. "I wouldn't miss seeing all of it," she assured him.

They walked outside onto a wooden deck and Megan gasped with appreciation.

"The backyard was overgrown, but it was what sold me," Mac said from beside her.

The expanse of grass and trees, surrounded by a fence and highlighted by a bubbling fountain in the center of a circular flower bed, cried out for a family. There was room for a swing set, a playhouse, even a pool, with plenty of space leftover for children to play tag in the grass.

"It's wonderful." Hands on the railing, Megan lifted her face to the gentle breeze that had sprung up. "You've made this into a real home, one with character and roots, not like so many new places that don't have any individuality."

He looked pleased by her comment. "That's exactly what I set out to do. I plan to live here for a long time."

There was a steadiness about him, a permanence she was beginning to admire, like the mountains forming a distant backdrop against the horizon. Suddenly Megan realized that Mac was going to make a good father to her child. She wanted to say so, but he had stopped by a nearby chaise lounge.

"Why don't you sit down. I'll get you something to drink and then I'll start the steaks. Lemonade?"

She sank onto the chair gratefully. "Sounds great. Can I do anything?" She hoped he'd say no. It felt good to put her feet up.

"There's nothing left to do." In moments he came back out with two tall, sweating glasses. "Steak and salad okay with you?"

"Wonderful." Sipping her lemonade, she watched him prepare their meal. He moved like a man who was used to feeding himself, efficient and relaxed. As the steaks sizzled on the grill, their aroma making her mouth water, he told her about reclaiming the backyard. Megan mentioned the blanket and baby clothes her cousin had sent. In no time the meat was ready.

Mac was disappointed when Megan only picked at her dinner. She insisted that it was done to her liking and apologized for not being more hungry.

"Don't worry about it," he said, trying to put her at ease. She looked a little pale and that tension he'd noticed when she arrived was back in her expression.

To relax her, he asked about her plans for after the baby came.

"That's the nice thing about working at home," she said, dividing a tomato wedge into small pieces. "I've made arrangements to cut down on my commitments for a month or two, and I can always work when the baby's napping. I won't have to worry about daycare at all."

Mac was glad the tyke wouldn't be stuck with a baby-sitter. Although he had no experience at all with small children, he hoped that, in time, the child could go on outings with him. Mac could probably impose his rights, but he would much rather she agreed voluntarily.

"Will you let me be there when you deliver?" he asked cautiously as he cut into his steak. "I'm sure you'll have family with you, but it would mean a lot to me."

She bit her lip and glanced away. He assumed she'd refuse, but she appeared touched by his request.

"As your birth partner, I might actually be able to help you," he added quickly before he forked up a bite of meat.

When she didn't immediately reply, Mac figured she was trying to decide how to refuse politely. Knowing how much he could ask for before she retreated from him was like gentling a skittish horse.

"My relatives aren't coming," she said, surprising him. "I haven't even told them when I'm due." Her smile trembled at the corners. "I'd like you to be there."

Mac breathed a huge sigh of relief. "Count on it." He'd have four more classes in which to learn what to expect.

He was eating his salad, finally able to enjoy the meal, when Megan suddenly pushed back her chair.

"Bathroom break?" he teased.

She shook her head, her eyes wide with alarm as she glanced at his half-full plate.

"I'm sorry," she gasped, curling forward. "I think I'm in labor."

Two hours later, Megan was too tired to disagree when Mac insisted on taking her directly home instead of going back to his house to retrieve her car. All she wanted to do was to fall into bed.

The twinges she'd felt earlier had finally stopped and, after a quick exam, her doctor was certain they were a false alarm. Megan was embarrassed that she had ruined Mac's nice dinner and they'd both missed their class.

"I don't care if it was false labor," he told her as he escorted her to the door of her townhouse. "Since you don't want to stay in my guest room where I can keep an eye on you, I'll have someone bring your car back in the morning."

"Thank you." She had tried to apologize again and he waved it away. He'd been wonderfully solicitous and it was hard to keep herself from accepting the support he offered, but she was afraid that once she weakened she wouldn't be able to stop leaning on him when she'd finally have to.

He followed her inside and shut the door. "Are you sure you don't want me to sack out on your couch?" he offered with a dubious expression. "It looks long enough."

As much as she appreciated the suggestion, she didn't feel it was necessary. She needed time alone to regroup. "Dr. Gould said I'd be fine," she reminded him. ''And I already promised to call you if anything else happens.''

''Anything at all,'' he insisted. He'd been hovering over her since she'd first made her startling announcement. All she'd been able to think of at the time was that it was too soon, and she still had so much to do! She'd been relieved when the doctor had assured her he thought she'd go full term.

''Take it easy,'' he'd cautioned before he let her leave. ''And call me if you have more contractions or any concerns at all.'' Then he'd turned her over to Mac, whom she had introduced as the baby's father. The two men had exchanged a look of masculine commiseration over Megan's head, making her feel like a flighty female who had to be carefully watched. She'd grumbled as much to Mac on the way to his truck.

''Maybe the doctor was just happy to see that you weren't dealing with this alone,'' he'd suggested diplomatically as he helped her into the cab. ''And maybe I enjoy keeping an eye on you,'' he'd added with a wink.

''Are you into whale watching, too?'' she'd muttered at the time, eliciting a snort of laughter followed by a hasty denial.

His mild flirting was a balm to her ego. Maybe letting him into her life wouldn't prove to be a big mistake, just as long as she maintained control—and managed to keep from falling for him.

It wouldn't do to complicate an already difficult situation. For the baby's sake, what they needed to establish was a rock-solid relationship based on trust and mutual respect, not one formed on the shifting sand of temporary sexual attraction. Provided Mac didn't kiss her again, she might be able to prevent what would surely be a major disaster for all three of them.

At his house, Mac paced the length of the deck and back, unable to sleep. He'd already dealt with the remnants of their abandoned dinner, cleaned the grill and fed the leftover steak to the appreciative dog.

What Mac should be doing now was reviewing the chapter on delivery in the book Megan had dropped off at his office. He hadn't realized until she made her dramatic announcement earlier just how unprepared he really was. Although he'd struggled to hide his blind panic with a veneer of calm reassurance, she'd scared the hell out of him. And now there was no guarantee they'd have time for the class covering this rather vital segment before she really did give birth.

Mac suspected there was a foolish grin plastered on his face at the idea, and he was glad his neighbors lived too far away to see it, even if they should be up at this ungodly hour. For a moment he tried to picture the infant. Would it have Megan's eyes? His chin? His father's nose, poor thing? Brown hair or tresses the color of wild honey?

He squeezed his eyes shut as unexpected emotion swept through him, leaving him shaken.

For the first time in years, Mac regretted having quit smoking. Even Rusty, full of U.S. Grade A beef scraps, had abandoned him to snore softly beneath the dining room table. Mac drained the beer he'd brought outside. Overhead a shooting star etched a path in the night sky and he uttered a brief prayer for the child's health.

Too bad it was so late. He could have made that call to his mother and father he'd been postponing—the one telling them they were about to be grandparents.

Mac frowned at the darkness beyond the deck. The only light came from behind him in the kitchen. The person he really wanted to call was Megan, but he knew—or at least he hoped—that she was getting some much needed rest.

Until today he'd never thought about the purely physical toll pregnancy must take on a woman's body. It had to be tough, and scary, but Megan believed a baby was worth the effort.

He shook his head. He knew the importance of an heir to pass on the family name, the Duncan bloodline, but she hadn't said much about her family, so why? He'd kissed her, but she was still an enigma.

Mac wandered back inside and tossed his empty beer bottle into the trash. The events earlier in the evening had been a wake-up call. They were having a baby. One minute he'd been considering whether or not he could resist kissing Megan again before they left for class, the next he'd been rushing her to the clinic. At least her O.B. had met her there right away, leaving Mac to cool his heels in the waiting room. After what had only seemed like an eternity, the doctor had escorted her out with instructions to take it easy and call him if anything changed.

Megan had actually tried to apologize to Mac for ruining his dinner!

Still wide awake, he knew he'd better get some rest or he'd be useless to Megan if she needed him again. And need him again she would. He was determined to be a part of her life. Except that his motives, so clear at first, had somewhere along the line become muddled. Was it the child that Mac wanted so desperately to know, or the mother?

"I want to go on record that I don't think this is a good idea," Mac said. "You should be resting."

"Nonsense." It wasn't Megan's fault he'd insisted on driving her to the next class, or that she had errands to run on the way. Right now they were leaving the local drugstore with a bag of baby supplies she refused to go one more day without.

"I offered to meet you at the clinic," she reminded him as they walked back to his pickup. "I'm not an invalid." Even if her ankles were swollen and her sandals too tight for her puffy feet.

In the week since the false alarm, Mac had taken to calling her several times a day. He'd even showed up at her townhouse with lunch on two separate occasions. Her only real disappointment was that neither time had he been inclined to kiss her. That one passionate embrace must have been a fluke, an impulse on his part that he'd since regretted.

Who could blame him? He'd barely be able to fit his arms around her now. The baby had dropped, making Megan feel as though she'd put on another thirty pounds overnight.

"Oh, oh," Mac groaned as she preceded him to the passenger side of his truck.

She turned expectantly. "What's wrong?"

Another couple was coming toward them, the man smiling expectantly at Mac. "Hey, buddy!" he exclaimed, curving his arm possessively around his companion's shoulders, "How goes?" His hair was shot through with gray and the woman with him was a striking brunette who made Megan feel like a brood mare.

"Dennis Reid," Mac muttered to Megan even as he returned the other man's smile. The two couples exchanged introductions. The way Dennis was hanging all over the other woman, whose name was Rachel Arquette, made Megan uncomfortable. Rachel, obviously a lot younger than Dennis, didn't appear to be all that keen about his attention, either.

"When's your baby due?" she asked Megan, smiling warmly.

"A couple of weeks." Now that Megan knew who Dennis was, she was tempted to complain to him about the way the clinic had mishandled her case.

Of course if they hadn't screwed up, Mac wouldn't be standing here beside her right now. She would never have met him. The realization was a sobering one, her reaction mixed.

"Rachel and I have been talking about taking a little trip down to Mexico," Dennis was telling Mac.

"*Dennis* has been talking about it," Rachel corrected him, an edge to her voice.

His laugh sounded forced. "She'll go. She can't resist me."

It was obvious to Megan that the only one who believed that was Dennis. Rachel was pretty enough to have any man she wanted, but perhaps she was attracted to his position of authority. They seemed like an odd couple, and there was something about her—

"Speaking of going," Mac said with a glance at Megan, "we've got a childbirth class to attend." After polite goodbyes all around, he helped her into his pickup.

"Sorry about that," he said quietly. "Dennis can be a real pain."

"I think Rachel's pregnant," Megan blurted. "Is he the father? He was certainly doing his best to stake his claim."

Mac stared at her. "How should I know? I told you we play racquetball. We don't share confidences. And how could you tell? She didn't seem to, um, stick out anywhere."

Like me? Megan wanted to ask. "Trust me," she

said instead. "Maybe it takes one to know one, but I'd say Nurse Arquette is definitely in the family way."

When Mac took her home after their class, he hoped she would invite him in and she did. They needed to talk. There was a lot he still didn't know about her.

"Want some coffee or a beer?" she asked after she'd shown him to the living room.

Mac opted for a brew to make it easier on her. She looked tired and he'd noticed how she limped as though her feet were sore. He should be unselfish and leave, but he wasn't going just yet.

Bringing his choice and a glass of water for herself, Megan joined him on the couch. When she kicked off her sandals, he bent down and lifted her bare feet into his lap.

She looked surprised, but she didn't object, even when he began massaging the ball of one foot. As he worked his way toward her ankle, smoothing away the knots of tension, she leaned her head back, eyes closed, and moaned low in her throat.

The uninhibited sound scraped along his nerve endings with surprisingly erotic results, even as her full breasts drew his attention. Ignoring his body's howl of response, Mac switched his ministrations to her other foot.

"Feel good?" he asked as her eyelids fluttered.

In profile, her face was surprisingly sweet, her lashes thick as carpet fringe above nicely rounded cheeks and chin. Her lips, pale and naked, curved into a secretive smile. "Mmm," was her only response.

For several more long moments, he worked in silence as he watched the tension leave her face and tried to picture her before she'd gotten pregnant.

Even now she had a woman's ripe sexuality, not the fresh, dewy beauty of a girl, but something much more potent. Somehow he doubted she'd appreciate the distinction, so he kept it to himself. Deliberately he changed the touch of his hands as he shifted from kneading her ankle to caressing her calf.

Megan's eyes flew open and she straightened. Impulsively he leaned forward to meet her halfway.

Her taste was as sweet as he remembered. Instead of either pulling away or returning the kiss, she surprised him by staying perfectly still, mouth soft, as if she were absorbing every nuance of the experience. Then her lips parted and her hand stole up to wrap itself around the back of Mac's neck.

The blood roared in his ears and his heart thundered in his chest. His arousal was fast and insistent. He shifted, covering her more completely.

Her abdomen pressed against him and she squirmed. Sanity returned with a rush, like breaking through the ice and falling into the freezing water.

He jerked away as if she'd slapped him. "Did I hurt you?" His voice scraped like rusty metal.

Megan's cheeks were flushed, her eyes bright. "Do I look hurt?"

He shook his head, still dazed. She looked incredible.

Mac was staring down at her as though he'd done something shameful, Megan realized. Irritation replaced the desire humming through her. Unexpected tears filled her eyes.

Danged hormones!

His stunned expression turned puzzled, then horrified. "Don't cry!" he implored with typical macho terror of feminine weeping.

Instantly her tears evaporated. During their embrace her feet had gone from his lap to the floor. Now she stood so fast that dizziness threatened and she swayed. "I'm not crying!"

Mac leaped up and grabbed her arms. "Easy," he murmured, coaxing her back down to the couch. "You turned so pale I thought you were going to pass out on me."

"I'm fine," she snapped, shifting away from his grasp. Her emotions tumbled over and around each other like laundry in a clothes dryer—embarrassment, regret and frustration—and she refused to meet his gaze.

"I'm not sorry for kissing you," he said softly, "but I *am* sorry that I upset you."

"Why did you stop?" she demanded, finally looking at him. "Am I that repulsive?"

How was the poor man supposed to answer that?

Adding to her annoyance, he actually dared to grin. She could have slugged him, except that he looked so darned attractive. If she weren't pregnant, she would have climbed all over him.

If she weren't pregnant, he wouldn't be here. What a mood killer.

Mac's hand hovered over her stomach. "May I?" he asked.

Her head bobbed. Gaze locked on hers, he spread his palm against the bulge. The warmth of his touch soaked through the fabric.

"No," he said firmly, "nothing about you is repulsive, not the body that carries my child, not the breasts that will nourish it, and not the heart that already loves it."

Swallowing, Megan blinked back a fresh rush of tears. Then Mac surprised her further. He took her hand and placed it against his fly. Her eyes widened.

"Is it repulsive?" He asked, paraphrasing her question. His eyes searched hers.

Slowly Megan shook her head.

"Then I think you and I have a big problem."

Chapter Seven

Mac watched Megan carefully, trying to gauge her reaction to his statement. At least she hadn't cringed in disgust when he'd pressed her hand to him.

"It's only a problem if we make it one," she replied, blushing.

"What are you saying?" Mac asked. The last thing they needed at this point was more confusion.

She swallowed and the knuckles of her clasped hands paled as she clenched them together tightly. "I don't know why you'd be attracted to me in my condition."

Her comment surprised him. Couldn't she tell that he found her desirable? "Make no mistake, I *am* attracted."

He captured her chin in his fingers. Her eyes widened. Her lips were slightly parted and tempting as hell. For an instant he debated presenting her with a list of reasons, but he discarded the idea. How could he explain what he himself didn't fully understand? "We're having a child together," he said instead. "And I think it's safe to say we get along?"

She nodded.

"So let's see where it leads. Is that okay with you?"

She searched his face and he wondered what she saw there. He was a pretty average guy, he thought, although Justine used to say the TV camera would love him, whatever that meant. Once Megan had the baby...

A tempting image of her popped into his imagination. Don't go there, he commanded himself.

"We have a lot to deal with right now," she finally said. "Can we take things slow? Is that okay with you?"

Gently he laid his hand against her stomach as mingled relief and apprehension poured through him. Was he simplifying the situation between them by acknowledging his desire for her or only complicating it?

"I don't think we have a choice," he said with a chuckle. "Slow seems to be our only current option."

Megan must have caught his meaning, because

her blush deepened and her gaze shifted away. "I guess you're right."

Mac slipped his arm around her shoulders and cuddled her closer, pleased when she relaxed against him. For several minutes he enjoyed the simple pleasure of merely holding her as he wondered what she was thinking.

When she remained silent, he let her go, angling around on the couch so he could watch her face. "I called my folks this morning." He'd caught them before they'd left the house, each listening on a separate extension once he had asked to speak to both of them.

His announcement had been met with stunned silence. As always, his first thought was that he had disappointed them yet again. Well, they'd wanted a grandchild and he was giving them one.

Recovering first, his mother had fired off a dozen questions for which Mac hadn't yet worked out answers. In the face of her inquisition, he'd decided against giving her too many details. When he was done fending her off, he'd ended up feeling cranky and defensive.

"Did you tell them?" Megan asked, looking up.

He knew she was referring to the special circumstances of their situation. "No, I figured they'd find out soon enough. They asked when junior is due. They wanted to know why I'd waited so long to tell them and why we haven't been to Denver so they could meet you."

His father had remained mostly quiet as usual,

except for a couple of sighs to let Mac know that once again his judgment had been found lacking. Only when he had confronted his father directly did he add his good wishes to those of Mac's mother.

"How did you respond?" Megan asked.

Mac patted her hand, trying to infuse reassurance. "They assumed our relationship must not have been serious until we found out you were pregnant. I'm afraid I didn't correct them."

To his relief, she didn't appear offended. "Can't get more casual than not even knowing each other at the time of conception," she quipped. Then her expression sobered. "Are they pleased about the baby, do you think?"

Mac shrugged. When had he ever made them happy? Relieved, perhaps, when he didn't screw up. Annoyed, surely, when he did, but *pleased?* Neither of them was demonstrative. How was he supposed to tell?

He didn't want to go into that now. "Happy enough, I guess. They want to meet you." To check her out, he suspected, but he didn't say that. No point in making her more nervous than she undoubtedly was already.

She stiffened at his comment. "Are they coming to Buttonwood?" Her tone was apprehensive.

"Not until you have the baby," he replied. How did he explain that their schedules were full, their lives too busy for two trips when one was sufficient?

At least Megan looked relieved and not disappointed. Then her eyes widened with horror.

"Are you telling me that I'm going to meet my baby's grandparents for the first time when I'm in labor?" she demanded. "Screaming like a wild woman, with sweaty hair and no makeup?"

"'Fraid so." Screaming? His courage wavered. No one had told him that having a baby involved any screaming. Putting aside his waffling courage, Mac hauled her back into his arms and patted her shoulder.

"It will be fine," he soothed, hoping like mad that he was right. Would his parents' eternal disappointment in him extend to Megan and the baby as well? Often enough he'd heard them discount someone who hadn't graduated from a prestigious college, and as far as he knew, Megan hadn't even attended a public university.

Well, perhaps the arrival of a little Duncan would be enough to stave off too close an examination of her background, as well as more questions like those he had dodged over the phone. Knowing his mother, though, there was no way on earth she would allow him to evade her a second time.

"We'll have to work out what to tell them so we don't trip each other up," he said.

"The truth is usually the best choice." Megan's tone was slightly disapproving. "Otherwise one of us is bound to make a slip."

"You're right, of course. I'll explain the situation when I see them." Perhaps by then, he thought, it will have changed. He and Megan had certainly taken a couple of tentative steps this evening.

Mac didn't stop to analyze the possessiveness that surged through him. He wanted his baby and he wanted Megan. For now that was enough for him to contend with.

"I hope I don't disappoint them," she murmured.

He shrugged. "Everything I do disappoints them in some way. They'll get over it." Damn, he hadn't meant to say all that. He'd finally stopped trying to please them a decade ago, when he'd quit the architectural firm and moved to Buttonwood.

Megan looked puzzled. "I assumed you were very close."

Had he led her to believe that? In order to defuse her concern about making a good impression, honesty compelled him to attempt an explanation.

"I interrupted their well-ordered lives. Academia was their world. The noise and dirt a little boy generates had no place there." He frowned, thinking back. "My parents admire intellect, structure, correctness, and the pursuit of culture—music, the arts. They insist on discipline, certainly, and self-control. Ambition, as long as it's tasteful. Not sports and of course nothing as crude as manual labor." He broke off abruptly. From what deep well of resentment had that all sprung?

"Don't get me wrong," he added when she remained silent. "My life was hardly deprived. My parents are both successful in their respective fields. I lacked nothing.''

"Nothing material?'' she guessed. ''What about love and warmth and acceptance?''

"Did you have all that?'' he countered. ''You certainly haven't indicated that you did.''

She frowned. ''I don't like to talk about that part of my life, but let me assure you that this baby—'' she patted her stomach ''—will have plenty of love.'' She pursed her lips. ''Do your parents have a good marriage? Are they still in love?''

It was Mac's turn to frown. What on earth was she getting at? ''They respect each other,'' he replied. ''They get along. Unlike some of my friends' parents, they never shouted that I can remember, never indulged in name calling, and of course they never came to blows.'' He could remember his father's chilly disapproval, much more stinging than a slap, and his mother's endless cautions that he not muss her clothes or hair. Had his father been allowed to muss her up? Mac doubted it.

"Why do you ask?'' he demanded when he realized that once again he's said more than he meant to. ''If you're afraid they'll turn into doting, interfering grandparents, put the idea straight out of your head. Their lives are far too busy for that. They seldom make the trek down from Denver and I'm sure they won't suddenly become pests, if that's your worry.''

In truth, they'd been to his house exactly once, shortly after he first bought the place. It had been too rundown and dated for his mother's taste, and his father pronounced it a poor investment. Neither of them had been interested in visiting Small World, so Mac hadn't made a big deal about it.

"I'm not worried." Megan pleated the hem of her shirt with her fingers.

"What then?" He didn't like the way the conversation was going. He wanted to find out more about her, not bare his soul for her scrutiny.

"I'm afraid our baby and I will learn to count on you," she said softly. "Then you'll meet someone else and fall in love. You'll want babies of your own, with her. What then?"

Mac didn't want her deciding she and junior would both be better off without him. "If I have other children, they won't mean any more to me than this one," he said, taking her hand. "How could I forget my firstborn?" Or its mother, he thought, staring deep into her eyes.

Her irises, he had noticed before, were changeable, like the colors reflected in the pond behind his house. Sometimes they were mostly blue; at others they appeared to be gray. Tonight they were green, with a band of gold around each pupil, like a halo. They were narrowed with concern.

"Things change," she said. "People change. You fall in love—"

"Pardon me if I don't go for all that romantic claptrap," he cut in briskly as he dropped her hand. "People get married, they become a team with common goals and shared interests. They support each other. It's a practical arrangement.'' He shrugged. ''Sure, passion plays a part, but you can keep it in perspective.''

He thought of his parents. He'd never heard them raise their voices, never seen them in a passionate embrace, but they had security. Then he recalled the kiss he and Megan had shared.

''Believe me,'' he vowed, ''I'm in no danger of losing my head over anyone.'' He hoped he'd managed to reassure her, but he could swear he saw disappointment, even sadness, flicker across her face.

''What's wrong now?'' he demanded, exasperated. ''Haven't I convinced you yet?''

''Most definitely,'' she said in an odd tone as she got to her feet. ''You've done an excellent job. Now I hate to toss you out, but if you've finished that beer, it's probably time you went home.''

Mac shot to his feet and stared down at her, but she didn't meet his gaze. Women! How could any mere male be expected to understand them? And the pregnant ones had to be the worst.

He felt as though he'd been going around in circles, like an out-of-control top, spinning and spinning. Now he was dizzy with confusion and uncertainty. Earlier he'd thought they had come to an understanding of sorts. Now he was standing on quicksand.

Unwilling to crawl away without one last attempt to reestablish some level of intimacy between them, he took her in his arms. She tensed up, increasing his irritation, and her gaze flew to his.

Now he had her attention! Determined, he bent his head and kissed her, intending to give her something to think about after he left. The moment her lips softened and her arms slid around his waist, he realized his plan had backfired. That was the last coherent thought he had for several moments. When he finally let her go, his body was throbbing like the bass from a cranked-up car stereo.

''Good night,'' he muttered as he brushed past her and headed for the door, unsure whether he was the victor in that last encounter, or the vanquished.

Megan was still thinking about their conversation and what followed the next afternoon. She'd been staring idly at her computer monitor for so long that the screen saver had come up. Concentrating on mousses and soufflés was difficult after finding out the man she was falling for didn't believe in love.

After growing up without it, she'd made up her mind to settle for nothing less than the complete romantic package Mac swore didn't exist. How could he kiss her the way he had and not recognize the magic Megan could feel sizzling between them?

For a little while she had started to believe he was capable of loving their child, even loving her. After the way he'd described his own childhood, she wasn't so sure he was capable of either. If she wasn't careful, an innocent baby could be hurt because she let her emotions usurp her common sense.

Megan had finally managed to focus her attention on a recipe for apricot soufflé with brandy sauce when her doorbell rang. Hoping it was Mac, she made her way carefully down the stairs.

When she got to the door, Blanche Hastings was waiting with a smile. "I'm so glad you're home," she said. "We need you to come over to the complex meeting room right away."

"I'm working," Megan protested. "What's so urgent?"

"The homeowners' association is deciding on whether to replace the mailboxes with ones that lock. We need another member present to make the vote legal," Blanche explained. "Come on, it will only take a couple of minutes."

Megan glanced down at the oversized man's T-shirt she was wearing with wrinkled shorts and no shoes. She hadn't bothered with makeup and her hair was lank. The day was muggy and her energy was nonexistent, unlike Blanche, who appeared ready to polka back down the sidewalk. Just looking at her, gray hair elaborately styled, outfit color-coordinated with her tennis shoes, made Megan tired.

"I really shouldn't," she began.

"Nonsense. This is important." Blanche was on the board of the condo homeowners' association, and she took her position very seriously.

"Can't you get anyone else?" Megan asked half-heartedly. Going with Blanche would probably take less time than arguing. The older woman didn't appear willing to take no for an answer.

"Everyone else who isn't at work is already there." Blanche folded her arms and waited expectantly.

Megan wanted to remind her that she, too, had a job. "Oh, all right," she said instead. "Let me grab my house key and some shoes." She thought about lipstick and running a brush through her hair, but Blanche was tapping her foot. Megan locked her front door and followed her neighbor across the grassy common area.

After a moment Blanche glanced over her shoulder and immediately slowed her steps to match Megan's. Since the baby had dropped, waddling was her main mode of transportation.

"Sorry, dearie," Blanche said with a tinkling laugh. "It's been a while since I was in the family way, and I've forgotten how it slows you down."

Megan dragged out a tight smile. "I'm okay." Quick, she was thinking, I want to make this quick and get back home. Maybe a nap would discourage the headache she could feel gathering behind her eyes like storm clouds on the horizon.

When they approached the meeting room, she got a glimpse of several women through the window. Good grief, how many did they need to pass a simple vote? Megan had meant to get more involved with the governing of the complex, but so far she just hadn't found the time.

Her first hint that something wasn't right was the

pink and blue crepe-paper streamers cascading down from the central light fixture. The second was the sheet cake on the side table, decorated with a border of bright yellow baby ducks.

She turned to Blanche as the cry went up.

"Surprise! Surprise!"

"Gotcha," Blanche told her, eyes twinkling above a rather smug grin.

Trying to keep her dismay from showing, Megan glanced around the circle of faces. There was Blanche's cohort, Flo Harris, Megan's friends Patty and Jill, several other neighbors she had met over the last few months, and Millie Johnson from Mom & Pop's, the local diner.

Patty and Jill rushed up to give Megan hugs.

"Couldn't you have warned me?" Megan hissed into Patty's ear.

"Don't be upset," Patty whispered back with an unrepentant grin. She, of course, had come from work and didn't look like a field hand. "Stopping Blanche is like keeping the Titanic from sinking. Might as well go down partying."

Before Megan had a chance to reply, Blanche grabbed her elbow. "As soon as you say hello to everyone, you can open your presents and we'll cut the cake."

A short time later, Megan found herself sitting in the place of honor surrounded by piles of opened gifts, a bunch of balloons floating from the back of her chair and a paper plate balanced on her knees. Someone had thrust a cup of punch into her hand.

Flo had pinned a ribbon corsage onto her faded T-shirt while Blanche took pictures.

So far no one had mentioned the baby's father, and Megan was starting to relax. It was really sweet of them to go to all this trouble.

"My daughter Janice is a nurse at the baby clinic," Mrs. Bailey, another neighbor, announced from Megan's right.

Instantly she stiffened. Was she about to be exposed?

"Janice told me one of the other nurses is in a family way. They think the chief of staff is the father," the woman continued.

A blue-haired lady on her other side made a tsking sound. "I don't understand these young people who insist on having babies outside of marriage," she exclaimed.

Blanche cleared her throat noisily. The old lady glanced at Megan and then quickly ducked her head to concentrate on the contents of her paper plate.

There was an awkward silence, during which Megan realized the couple they'd been discussing was Mac's friend Dennis and the woman Megan had met and suspected was pregnant, Rachel Arquette.

"Are they getting married?" Flo asked, an avid expression on her lined face.

Mrs. Bailey shrugged. "According to my daughter, the nurse who's expecting had been seeing one of the other doctors, Colt Rollins, until he was transferred unexpectedly."

"I remember Dr. Rollins," someone volunteered. "He's very handsome and he looks a lot like one of the doctors on the soap I watch."

"Maybe the baby is his and not the other doctor's," Blanche suggested, joining the gossip session.

Relieved that their interest was diverted away from her, Megan nibbled on her cake, white with lemon filling to match the ducks on the frosting.

"Not the way the other fellow, Dr. Reid, is talking," Mrs. Bailey said. "It sounds as though he's taking *all* the credit."

From what Mac had said about Dennis, Megan could picture him doing that, whether or not the baby was actually his. She'd gotten the impression when she'd met him and Rachel that they weren't all that close. The pretty brunette didn't seem to appreciate his possessiveness. How sad for the woman if the father of her baby was really the other doctor, the one who had gone somewhere else.

"Maybe she doesn't know who the father is," Flo said and the blue-haired lady gasped.

Megan glanced at the big wall clock. Surely no one would be offended if she pleaded fatigue and slipped away. Patty and Jill had gone back to their respective jobs as soon as the gifts had been opened and the others had either already left or were still sitting around talking.

Heaving herself to her feet, Megan approached Blanche and Flo, who had just begun to clean up the mess.

"Can I help?" Megan asked.

Flo looked shocked. "Of course not. The party was for you. The guest of honor doesn't do KP."

"I can't thank you enough," Megan told them both. "It was very sweet."

"Were you surprised?" Blanche demanded after she'd dumped a stack of dirty plates into the trash.

"Completely," Megan answered truthfully. She'd been far too preoccupied with thoughts about Mac to be at all suspicious when Blanche dragged her to the meeting room, but she didn't figure it would be polite to say so.

"You got some nice things for the baby," Blanche added, glancing at the presents. "I hope you can use the swing." She and several of the other neighbors had gone together on a wind-up swing that rocked the baby while it played music.

"I'm sure it will come in very handy," Megan replied, wondering if she could get Mac to come and get it for her later.

"You're looking pale," Flo said. "Why don't you go on home? We'll see that everything gets delivered."

Grateful, Megan thanked them again, said a quick goodbye to the women who were still sitting around gossiping, and left. Even though she had originally avoided the idea of a baby shower, it had been rather fun. She'd gotten some nice gifts for the baby—a couple of cute sun-suits, a bonnet, a stuffed lamb, a tiny pair of sandals, a package of terry washcloths, a rattle and a basket that had drawn a round of laughter when she unwrapped it. Inside was soap, powder and lotion for the baby, earplugs, aspirin and Godiva chocolates for Megan, as well as a small package that made her blush.

She was looking forward to telling Mac about the shower and what she'd heard about Dennis and Rachel. It wasn't that she enjoyed repeating gossip, she told herself, she just wanted him to know her hunch about Rachel had been correct.

When she turned the corner by her unit, she was surprised to see Mac hurrying toward her. He was wearing cutoff jeans that showed off his muscular legs, a Broncos T-shirt and a baseball cap. It wasn't fair that, even dressed the way he was, he still managed to look good while Megan felt like an unmade bed.

When he spotted her, his frown deepened. Despite the sunglasses covering his eyes, she could tell something was wrong.

"What is it?" she asked. "Are you okay?"

Mac walked right up to her and captured her elbow in one hand. His mouth was set in a grim line and she wished she could read the expression his eyes, but the dark lenses formed an impenetrable shield.

"Where have you been?" he demanded without so much as a preliminary greeting. "I've been calling you for two hours and I was just about to ring your bell when I spotted you walking over here. I expected to find you passed out on your bathroom floor.'' He glanced down at her chest. ''What the hell is that?''

She'd forgotten to unpin the makeshift corsage. ''It's the bows from my shower,'' she snapped, hackles lifting at his tone. ''I suppose you'd better come inside,'' she added ungraciously.

Although there was no one around, Mac hadn't bothered to lower his voice and she was very conscious of the open windows facing the central common area. If they were about to have their first argument, she preferred to do it without potential witnesses.

As soon as she had shut her front door behind them, she turned on him. Her mellow mood had evaporated, replaced by a return of her earlier frustration over his attitude toward love.

''Don't you ever talk to me that way again,'' she warned, slapping her palms against his chest and shoving him. ''What on earth is your problem anyway?''

Mac's head jerked back and his sunglasses slid down his nose. Pulling them off, he jammed them into his chest pocket as he took an involuntary step away from her.

''I was worried about you,'' he shouted, the tips of his ears turning red. ''When I couldn't reach you by phone, I walked out on my crew and raced over here like a damned idiot.'' His expression was thunderous, his dark eyes snapping with anger. ''I'm lucky not to have gotten a speeding ticket.''

Megan could see a sprinkling of sawdust on the

front of his T-shirt. There was a smear of dirt on his cheek, beads of moisture on his forehead and a streak of green paint on one forearm. He looked like the poster boy for sweaty sex.

As quickly as it had come, Megan's annoyance dissipated. "I'm sorry you were worried," she said in a quieter voice. "Some of my neighbors threw me a surprise baby shower over in the meeting room."

Mac's face turned a dull red and he glanced around as though he were searching for someplace to hide. Then he took off his cap and raked his fingers through his hair, leaving it in untidy furrows.

"Damn, I'm sorry."

"Don't be. It was actually kind of fun and I got some nice presents."

His eyes narrowed. "You know I didn't mean I was sorry about the shower," he grumbled, jamming his cap back on his head.

Megan had no choice but to take pity on him. "Would you like a beer?" She'd gotten a six-pack just the other day in case he came over.

He shook his head. "No, thanks. I have to get back to work. Got any of that iced tea before I go?"

"No, but I do have lemonade."

His frown relaxed ever so slightly. "That would be great." He followed her to the kitchen like an overgrown puppy and plopped himself down on one of the barstools facing her across the expanse of counter.

"Can we start over?" he asked in a subdued voice.

Megan handed him a tall glass of lemonade and ice. "I'm not sure that's possible," she told him gravely.

The expression on his face would have been comical if he hadn't looked so devastated.

Chapter Eight

Mac paled. "What do you mean?" he asked hoarsely.

Oh, great. He'd come rushing over here because he thought Megan needed him and she'd taken advantage of his concern. She felt as low as the undercarriage on a VW Bug. "I'm sorry," she exclaimed, coming around the counter to lay her hand on his bare arm. "Of course we can start over, if that's what you want, but the baby's due shortly. Do we really have time?"

He stared uncomprehendingly at her attempt at humor.

"I'm kidding," she said. "Thank you for worrying about me."

Mac's expression finally cleared. "Kiss and make up?" he asked with a rakish grin.

Megan closed her eyes, puckered up and leaned forward expectantly. Nothing happened. Embarrassed, she opened her eyes again.

Mac hadn't moved, but he was staring at her as though she'd just grown a second set of ears.

"What's wrong?" she asked.

"Not a damn thing." His voice was husky. Gently he cupped her chin in his big, strong hand. His eyes were as dark as Belgian chocolate, his gaze intent.

Slowly he leaned forward and laid his mouth against hers. The kiss he gave her was so tender that it made her insides flutter. When he released her, she drew in a shaky breath. How could this complex, caring, solitary man claim that love didn't exist?

For their baby's sake and her own heart, it was up to Megan to show him it did.

He cleared his throat and turned back to his lemonade. "Tell me about the shower," he suggested as he tipped back his glass. "Did you get a lot of loot?"

"When's the baby scheduled to arrive?" Elaine asked. A few moments before, she'd brought two cups of coffee into Mac's office, handing one to him and sitting in the chair facing his desk. She had caught him in a weak moment and he ended up telling her all about Megan. Talking to someone was a relief.

"Megan's not due for a week yet," he replied. "The doctor says everything is progressing right on schedule."

"First babies come early," Elaine warned, crossing her legs. She had three boys of her own. "I hope you're prepared."

Prepared? "Is anyone ever really ready for this?" he asked dryly. He would have liked to finish the entire course on childbirth, but he'd known all along they'd miss the last few sessions. Even though he'd read several books on the subject, there was still so much he didn't know. Diapering a doll wasn't quite the same as holding a tiny little being that breathed and cried and needed constant care.

"I'm scared to death," he admitted to Elaine.

She emitted a sharp bubble of laughter. "Welcome to parenthood."

He called Megan every morning to check on her and he went by there each evening they didn't have class. The day after her shower, when he'd seen how tired she looked, he'd hired a cleaning lady to visit her townhouse twice a week. Megan was in no shape to scrub toilets and push a vacuum. At first she'd argued, and then she had insisted on paying the agency herself.

She was so damned scared of losing her independence, but he was determined to make a place for himself in her life.

"Are you thinking about marrying this woman?"

Elaine asked boldly, scattering his thoughts like Lego blocks.

Mac would freeze out anyone else who dared to ask such a personal question, but Elaine had been his first employee in Buttonwood. At the time she had just gone through a difficult divorce. Although she had a business background, she hadn't worked in years, her self-confidence was non-existent and she knew nothing about computers.

Mac hadn't been certain he could turn a sideline into a successful business. They'd taken a chance on each other, setting up shop in a rundown building. He'd paid for her computer training, her first desk had been a card table and now, a decade later, he liked to think they were friends. Her children had worked for him during their summer vacations and now the oldest was an architecture major at the University of Colorado.

Mac realized that Elaine was still waiting for him to reply. "Marriage is a big step," he hedged, taking a sip of the excellent coffee.

"So's having a baby."

"I explained how that happened," he protested. "It was all a mistake."

"And that's how you'll explain it to your son or daughter when they're old enough to understand? Provided you haven't lost touch by then?"

"I won't abandon my child," Mac said stubbornly. After her divorce, Elaine's ex-husband had left the state. He sent her money, but he hadn't visited the boys in years. Mac and Elaine's brother filled in the best they could.

"What if Megan moves away?" Elaine asked, setting her mug on the edge of his desk. "Eventually she may. What if she marries someone else? She's an attractive woman and she's certainly young enough to have more children—the family you said she's never had."

Mac had told Elaine what little he knew about Megan's background. Now he struggled with the silent protest that swelled inside him. It wasn't just the idea of a stepfather raising his child that sent a shaft of pain through Mac, he realized with a shock. It was the image of Megan belonging to another man, a *husband*.

Elaine was watching him closely, making him wonder how much of his sudden insight showed on his face. The woman was like a badger when it came to digging out secrets. Until now, he hadn't thought about marrying Megan.

The phone on his desk rang, startling both him and Elaine. Automatically she reached over and plucked the receiver from its cradle.

"Good afternoon, Small World." She glanced at Mac. "Hold on, he's right here." Handing him the phone, she said quietly, "It's Megan. She sounds upset."

When Megan heard Mac's voice, her body sagged with relief. She had always planned on driving herself to the clinic when her time came, but he'd pitched a fit when she said so. Finally she had given him her word that she would at least try to reach him before she left and now she was so glad she had.

She'd felt the first twinges very early this morning when they woke her from a sound sleep, but it had taken a while for her to recognize their significance. For several hours she'd been in denial. It was too soon. She wasn't ready. Now that the time had actually come and the doctor insisted she go to the clinic, her sudden burst of apprehension had caught her totally unprepared.

What had she been thinking, deciding to raise a baby by herself?

She'd even called her cousin, Wendy, and left a message on her machine. As soon as Megan hung up, she regretted the impulse, but she'd wanted to make contact with someone. Seeing the blanket draped over the crib had brought Wendy to mind. She'd tried to reach both Patty and Jill, but she was a week early and neither of her friends was around.

"Have you called the doctor?" Mac demanded. "How far apart are your contractions? Do you feel all right?"

"I'm okay," she said when he took a breath.

His voice sound shaky. Wasn't he supposed to be calming her down? "Don't leave. Don't do anything. I can be there in five minutes."

"Don't risk a speeding ticket," Megan replied. "I called Dr. Gould. My contractions are mild, about ten minutes apart." She hesitated, embarrassed. "There have been some other signs, but I feel great.'' Her overnight bag sat in the bedroom closet waiting for last-minute items. Good thing she'd made a list, because she was too distracted now to think straight.

"I still have some packing to do," she added, "and I want to feed Cassius before I go." The cat had been prowling restlessly all morning. He must have known something was up.

"Don't you dare lift that suitcase," Mac said. "I'll carry it for you when I get there."

The bag wasn't that heavy and she was no invalid, but Megan didn't bother to argue. Even though she'd told him not to hurry, she would feel much better after he got here.

"I'm leaving now," Mac added, voice climbing with excitement. Well, why not? All *he* had to do was hold her hand, remind her when to breathe and try not to faint. "I'll have my cell phone in the car if you need me. Do you have the number?"

"Yes, Mac. I'll try to manage until you get here," she said dryly, tempted to remind him that he was less than minutes away.

"Megan," he said, voice thick, and then he fell silent.

"What is it?" Perhaps he was having second thoughts. Maybe he resented being called away from work. No, he wouldn't let her down now. He'd stick it out, no matter how he felt. That was Mac, solid as a rock.

"It will be okay," he said as another contraction made her grip the receiver tighter. "We're going to do this together, just like we learned in class. Our baby will be fine.''

How had he known exactly what to say? Those pesky tears filled her eyes again. ''I know,'' she whispered, and then he broke the connection. After all the months of waiting, the preparations, second thoughts, changes in body shape and mood, the time had come to meet her child.

Megan replaced the phone. ''Happy birthday, baby,'' she said softly, head bowed.

As she stood at the window a few moments later, watching for Mac's pickup, Cassius wound his way between her ankles and meowed plaintively. He must have sensed her mood, anxiety and elation swirled together like chocolate-and-vanilla frozen yogurt in a waffle cone.

''Don't worry,'' Megan told the cat, bending carefully to pat its head. ''Mac will feed you and clean your box while I'm gone, and I'll be back before you know it.'' Wouldn't Cassius be surprised at what Megan was bringing home with her?

As she straightened, she saw an unfamiliar car pull into the parking area. It was barely stopped before Mac leaped out. At the sight of him, so dependable, so familiar in his plaid shirt and jeans, emotion swelled up into Megan's throat. She swallowed hard.

Hormones, she thought as she went to the door. Before she could get it open, Mac pounded thunderously. When she let him in, his expression was tight with concern as he looked her up and down.

"Doing okay?" he asked, giving her a hug before she could step aside.

Megan nodded against his shoulder, feeling the tension. "Thanks for coming so quickly."

"No problem." He let her go, concern edging the smile he produced for her benefit. Her white knight come to protect her.

Before she'd called him she had showered and slipped on a loose dress. Now she wished she'd done something with her hair and makeup, too. The thought nearly made her giggle out loud. They were having a baby and she was worried about her appearance. She had to be in love.

The thought sucked the air from her lungs as Mac grabbed her hand. A contraction hit, harder than the others, and she stiffened.

"Do you want me to call an ambulance?" he demanded.

"No, of course not. Where did you get the car?" she asked, trying to appear serene as the pain eased and she dealt with the enormity of everything bombarding her at once.

"What?" he asked, distracted. "Oh, the car? It's Elaine's. I thought you might want to lie down. I left her the keys to my truck."

Once again his thoughtfulness surprised Megan. He'd already hired a woman to clean her house and insisted on taking care of her cat. Was there no end to his concern? She remembered how, when he'd first contacted her, she had put off meeting him, worried he'd interfere in her life. Now she wondered how she would have managed these last weeks without his unwavering support. She'd have to tell him so, but not now.

"That's nice," she said instead. "Please thank Elaine for me."

He was looking around distractedly. "Is this your bag? Did you pack your CDs? M&M's?"

"All set," she said.

"Have you got your purse? Is everything shut off?" He peered at the kitchen. "Where's the cat?"

Megan hooked her arm through his. He wasn't as calm as he pretended to be. "Yes, yes, and under the bed. Now would you please stop worrying? People do this all the time."

He took a deep breath and studied her doubtfully, as though he expected her to explode like a big balloon. "If you say so."

At that moment another spasm rippled through Megan and she gasped softly. The muscles of Mac's arm went rigid.

"Contraction?" he asked.

"Mmm-hmm."

"Want to sit down?"

She shook her head.

He looked at his watch and waited for the spasm to pass. Once it did, he picked up her bag and she grabbed her purse. Giving her a quick peck on the lips, he said, "Let's get this show on the road."

Check-in at the clinic had gone smoothly, Mac thought a short time later. Megan was preregistered, so she'd been settled into a wheelchair right away, with him hovering uselessly at her side as they were escorted to the maternity wing. Now while Megan was getting comfortable, he took the time to call his parents and leave a message. He would have to ask Megan if she wanted him to contact anyone for her.

"Mr. Duncan, you can come in now," said a white-haired woman with "Nell" on her name tag and a clipboard in her hand.

Mac took a deep breath and followed her down the hall.

"I'm the midwife," she said over her shoulder. "Nervous? According to your file, you're a first-time daddy."

The word stopped him dead. "Yeah," he gasped, swallowing the panic rising in his throat. "First time." How had he thought he could do this?

Through the window he could see the back of Megan's head. She was already settled into a special chair and it looked as though she was using the phone. Maybe she didn't have any faith in him, either, and was already looking for reinforcements.

"We'll be right here to help," Nell told him. "Megan is dilated to four and her contractions are about five minutes apart."

"It's too soon," Mac argued. "She's not due for another week."

Nell's smile widened. "Trust me, it's time. A few hours from now, you'll be holding your new son or daughter. Meanwhile, Megan needs you."

Deliberately he recalled what he had learned in class. It would be his job to help her stay focused on her breathing, to encourage her and keep her relaxed, to time her contractions and get her whatever she needed.

"Are you ready?" Nell asked.

He gulped and nodded, wishing for a heartbeat that he was anywhere but here before shame washed over him. Megan was the one doing the real work. His job was the easy one.

"Stay positive," Nell said as she led the way into the labor room. It was just like the one he and Megan had toured during their second class together. How long ago that seemed now.

Megan concluded her call and looked up at Mac. She was pale and her eyes were huge. Instantly his own nervousness faded. "You'll be fine," he said, tucking a strand of her hair behind her ear.

She was hooked up to the fetal monitor and one of the tapes she'd brought was playing softly in the background. Flute music. For a moment, Mac watched the monitor, fascinated. It made everything more real.

Megan glanced at Nell, who immediately found something to do in the far corner of the room. "That was Patty on the phone. She has a bad cold and doesn't dare come anywhere near me." She sounded forlorn.

"I'm sorry," Mac replied. He knew that Megan had been counting on her friend's presence. "Is there anyone else I can call for you?"

Megan frowned. "No, not really. Jill's gone on a camping trip and won't be back until the day after tomorrow. She didn't want to go, but I insisted."

He pulled up another chair and took her hand in both of his. "Family?" he asked gently.

She shook her head.

"Are you sure?"

She nodded, chin high. He knew better than to persist. "What about your neighbors? The ones who threw your shower."

Megan plucked at her gown. "I'll call them later. Have you talked to your parents yet?"

"I left them a message just now, but I imagine they're still at the college."

She stiffened and the muscles of her jaw flexed. The contractions must be getting stronger. Carefully he laid one hand on her abdomen, stroking lightly, as he guided her breathing. Together they watched the fetal monitor as Mac wondered what she was thinking. Was she worried, elated, scared? He wished he could put his own feelings into words, but he'd never been good at describing them. Finally he felt the contraction ease and he withdrew his hand.

"Are they bad?" he asked.

"Not yet."

Nell brought her a cup of ice chips and several lollipops. "Keeps your mouth from getting too dry," she said. "Both of you."

For a while they stayed where they were, Mac coaching Megan's breathing through each contraction, massaging her feet, doing his best to distract her with small talk. He described at length the miniature castle he'd been designing, complete with its own drawbridge, and asked about the vegetarian cookbook she was indexing. After the first half-hour, he helped her to change positions.

"I've been thinking about names," she said when she was settled on her side, a cherry lollipop in her mouth. It gave her lips a red sheen that contrasted with the paleness of her face. "Do you have any preferences?"

Mac hadn't given the subject much thought, but now he wondered if the baby was going to be a Malone or a Duncan. "I never cared for juniors," he said, probing for some hint of her intentions. "So don't name it MacGregor."

"Not even if it's a girl?" she teased.

"Especially not if it's a girl." Together they dealt with another contraction.

"I like Tyler for a boy," she said, laying down the stick from her sucker. She got up and took a few steps, standing with her back braced against the wall. "Any objections?"

Tyler Duncan or Tyler Malone? Either one sounded okay to Mac, but what was wrong with John or Jim? He'd taken plenty of razzing in school over his own unusual moniker. "Tyler's okay," he said. "Have you picked a girl's name?"

She leaned against the wall and tipped back her head. "I don't know."

"Don't you think that's kind of long?" he blurted.

She looked startled and then she laughed. "Funny man," she gasped, bending forward. Immediately Mac went over and helped her back to the chair.

"What's your mother's name?" she asked when she was settled.

"Muriel."

"Oh." Her expression clearly showed her dismay.

Mac took pity on her. "She was named after her grandmother, but I'm not that crazy about the name."

"I'm sure we'll come up with something if we need to. You don't have to stay with me every minute, you know. Don't you want to go to the cafeteria or take a walk outside?" Her tone of voice had developed a sharp edge to it and he suspected she was feeling more uncomfortable.

"Trying to get rid of me?" he teased.

She shrugged. "You must be bored."

Mac reminded himself to be patient. Her face was shiny with perspiration and she tensed more with each new contraction. He wet the washcloth Nell had laid out and pressed it to Megan's forehead. "I'm not bored."

She shifted restlessly. "I don't want the music. Can we have the TV on?"

Wordlessly he picked up the remote and found a program he hoped would distract her. When Nell came in to do an internal exam, he paced outside in the hallway. When he came back, she had also started an IV, in case Megan changed her mind about taking a sedative or tranquilizer. So far she had refused.

"You're doing fine," Nell told them both. "Walk around a little if you want, but take it slow."

It was getting more difficult for Mac to watch Megan deal with the contractions. He wished she would accept some pain medication and he decided the old method of knocking the mother out during delivery was far more humane than this, as was keeping all the fathers together in some waiting room down the hall watching the big game on television. When he told Megan that, she choked out a laugh.

"I was just thinking the same thing," she replied. "Unconsciousness seems like a great idea right now."

Time crawled, while Mac told her what a great job she was doing. Megan rolled her eyes. Once she stuck out her tongue and she refused another lollipop. After a while, Nell checked her again. She disappeared for a few moments and when she came back, she helped Megan into the bed.

"Dr. Gould will be here shortly," she said as she began assembling towels and various instruments. "I've also alerted Dr. Davis. She's already in the hospital." Claire was the pediatrician who would examine the newborn.

"How much longer?" Mac demanded. Megan groaned softly with each contraction now, and she looked exhausted. Her hair was limp and there were dark patches beneath her eyes, which were unfocused when he spoke to her.

Nell laid a comforting hand on his shoulder. "Not long. Things will start moving pretty quickly now."

"Did you hear that?" Mac asked Megan, tone deliberately hearty. "Nell says our baby will be here soon."

"I heard her," Megan growled. "I'm not deaf."

Megan found Mac's sympathetic expression to be highly irritating. How dare he infer he knew what she was going through. No man could begin to understand!

Her contractions were coming much faster now and they lasted longer. She wondered how much more she could take before she was torn apart. At first they'd only been twinges, a fluttering sensation. Now they really hurt.

She couldn't even remember why she had thought having a baby would be a good idea. As another contraction ripped through her, she nearly cried out that she had changed her mind. She wanted this over. She wanted to go home.

"Hang in there," Mac whispered. "You're doing great. We're going to meet our baby real soon. This will all be worth it, you'll see."

Megan glared at him. He looked a little tired, but every hair was in place. He wasn't dripping with sweat and racked with pain. "Easy for you to say," she pointed out peevishly.

"You know if I could do this for you, I would."

For some reason, she believed him. Instantly she felt petty and mean. "I know," she mumbled, ducking her head. Then another contraction seized her, banishing her newfound goodwill. Silently she wished him and every other male on the planet straight to Hades.

"You're fully dilated, in the second stage of labor," Nell said after another brief exam.

With Mac's help, Megan adjusted her breathing so that it was more rapid and shallow. Her contractions seemed to drag on forever and she couldn't resist the urge to push down with each one. For a little while she stood up while Mac supported her. His words of encouragement were more automatic now, but Megan barely heard them. Her entire focus was on her own body and the baby struggling to be born.

Tears trickled from the corners of her eyes. Gently Mac wiped them away. "Good," he whispered, "you're doing good." His gaze was steady, his touch firm.

"I want to lie down," she said fretfully. No position felt good. None eased the pressure. Mac offered her ice chips, which she accepted gratefully even though a dry mouth was the least of her complaints.

"Help me get her back onto the bed," Nell told Mac. They waited until the next spasm of pain was over. After another quick check, Nell went to the wall phone.

In minutes Dr. Gould sailed into the delivery room. He smiled warmly at Megan and then at Mac. "How are you doing?" he asked.

"I changed my mind," Megan gasped between contractions.

"I'm afraid it's a little late for that." For some reason the reassuring smile she'd always found comforting now only irritated her. His teeth were too big, she noticed for the first time, and his mustache really needed a trim. Obviously he was unaware of her hostile thoughts. "It won't be long now."

The doctor performed his own examination as Mac hovered near the head of the bed. Any sense of modesty Megan had felt when she first came in was long gone. Her body had become public property. It wouldn't have surprised her if they'd run another class right through the delivery room while her gown was up around the mound of her belly.

"I hurt!" she exclaimed, struggling to remember everything she'd learned in class.

Dr. Gould's smile oozed phony sympathy. "I know, dear."

The hell he did! She contemplated popping him with her fist if he came within range, but she didn't have the strength. She hardly noticed when he motioned Mac to join him at the foot of the bed. As the door opened, she tilted her head back and saw Claire.

The pediatrician glanced at the fetal monitor and put a cool hand on Megan's forehead. "You're doing fine. The baby's fine. Not long now." She joined the others at party central.

"Push hard with the next contraction," Dr. Gould said, watching closely.

"My God," Mac exclaimed, "is that its head?"

Megan looked in the mirror. For a second, she lost focus on what she was doing. Then another contraction screamed through her. Nell squeezed her hand.

"Push, honey, that's the way," Mac said, staring intently.

Megan was entirely caught up in what was happening to her body. She pushed hard, groaning with the effort.

"That's it," Dr. Gould exclaimed. "Almost done. Now try to stop pushing. Let your baby come on its own."

Easy for you to say, Megan thought, struggling to comply. There was a moment of silence and then she heard a thin cry.

Mac looked up and smiled right at her, his eyes glimmering with moisture. "It's a boy," he said. "He's beautiful."

He hadn't thought the birth of his son would hit him so hard, he realized later as he sat on the corner of Megan's bed and watched her nursing Tyler. Mac should have been exhausted. Instead he was still high, as though he'd been breathing pure oxygen.

The baby was bald except for a dusting of nearly colorless fuzz and his skin had a golden tone instead of the pink Mac had expected, but he thought he recognized Megan's nose and chin, his father's ears.

Megan smoothed one finger down Tyler's tiny forearm. His tiny blue I.D. band matched the one on her wrist. "His head is shaped like yours."

"Pointed?" Mac teased.

"No, he's perfect," Megan insisted. "Aren't you, pumpkin?" she cooed.

Tyler made noisy, smacking sounds as he nursed. His hands, as small as a doll's, rested against her skin. Megan looked like a tired madonna. If anyone had told Mac he could stare at a woman's bare breast and not feel the faintest sexual jolt, he'd have laughed. Watching her nurture their child was an overwhelming experience, but it wasn't desire that swelled inside Mac like an outpouring of music. It was something just as strong, but different. Warmer, gentler, confusing as hell.

He ran his hand over the back of his neck. Seeing his newborn son with the woman who'd carried him all these months stirred up feelings of longing in Mac he couldn't begin to name or even understand.

Megan glanced up and must have noticed his slack-jawed stare. Her free hand went to her hair, patting it absently. While Tyler was getting checked over Mac had run a brush through it for her, but the ends stuck out every-which-way.

"What is it?" she asked, clearly puzzled.

"You're beautiful," Mac said hoarsely. Hand unsteady, he stroked a finger across Tyler's head, so small and fragile, like a bird's egg. The baby jerked at his touch and then settled back to nursing.

Megan's smile was nearly as wide as it had been when he'd first placed the squirming infant on her stomach. "You're crazy." Her voice was hushed, her expression dreamy as she gazed at their child with her heart in her eyes. Mac wondered if anyone had ever looked at him that way. For a moment he felt unbearably lonely, but he shook it off. His parents loved him. They just weren't demonstrative people.

"Have I thanked you?" he asked Megan, forcing the words past the lump of contentment in his throat. He'd have to call Elaine, and maybe try his parents again, but not just yet. It was getting late. He'd have to get some sleep. Megan, too, needed her rest, but he hated to leave her.

"No thanks needed." For a long moment he and Megan stared at each other, then Tyler made a sound. Instantly her attention shifted. His head bobbed and he frowned up at her, his forehead as wrinkled as a wise old man's.

"All done?" She burped him gently. The sound he emitted, so out of proportion to his size, made Mac laugh.

He could have watched them for hours, but a

nurse came in to take Tyler to the nursery so Megan could get some rest. She gave him up with obvious reluctance.

As the nurse went back out, Dr. Davis came in. She'd done a quick exam in the delivery room just a few minutes after Tyler was born. Mac hadn't seen her since and now she looked tired as she tucked a chart under her arm and greeted them both.

"This has been a long day for you," Mac commented. "Is everything all right?"

Megan sat up straighter. "What is it?" her voice rose and he could hear the fear in it. "Is Tyler okay?" Instinctively Mac leaned over and took her hand in his.

"It's not uncommon for newborns to be slightly jaundiced at birth," the doctor said quickly, "so I don't want you to worry. Tyler's TSB level is a little higher than we'd like, but we aren't too concerned at this point."

"If it's too high, can you lower it?" Mac asked, fear squeezing his gut like a big hand. What if something was seriously wrong?

"Most babies will clear excess bilirubin, which is what causes the symptoms, on their own. If it's not down after 24 hours, we'll use Phototherapy, which basically means we'll put him under some special lights. In addition, we'll have you breast feed him more often to help flush his system."

"And what if that doesn't take care of the problem?" Megan asked.

"In extreme cases, a transfusion may be required,'' the doctor admitted. ''But we aren't even considering that at this point, so let's not get ahead of ourselves. Like I said, neonatal jaundice is quite common.'' She patted Megan's arm and gave Mac a smile that was meant to be reassuring. ''We'll be watching him carefully and I'll keep you posted on his progress.''

''I can give blood if he needs it,'' Mac blurted.

She smiled. ''I don't foresee that being necessary, but I'll keep it in mind.''

After she left, Mac squeezed Megan's hand tighter before he let it go, sure his face mirrored the concern he saw in hers. Never had he experienced such a depth of feeling for another human being as he did now, for his son.

''He'll be fine,'' Megan told him, eyes brimming with tears and worry.

He dug deep for the reassurance he knew she needed. ''Of course he will. He's a tough little guy and Dr. Davis is the best. Let's not borrow trouble.''

He was about to add something, anything, when the door swung open and two people peered inside.

''Dad!'' Mac exclaimed as he hopped off the bed with a touch of self-consciousness. ''Mother.''

Chapter Nine

Megan stared at the couple standing in the doorway to her hospital room. She could see no similarity to Mac in his mother's thin face or stylish blond bob, and only a faint resemblance in his aesthetic-appearing father with his short gray hair and glasses.

"Come in," Mac said, extending a hand to the older man, who pumped it once and released it. His mother, wearing a severe black suit and pearls, leaned forward to rest her hands briefly on his shoulders and kiss the air near his cheek.

"Hello, darling. Have we come at a bad time?" She glanced pointedly at his rumpled clothing. In stark contrast to his father's suit and tie, Mac was still wearing the same shirt and jeans he'd had on when he picked Megan up hours before and his jaw was dark with stubble.

"We've been having a baby," Mac said dryly. "Please excuse my appearance. There hasn't been time to clean up."

Megan would have liked nothing better than to dive under the covers until they left. After her nap she had washed her face, but it was as bare as Tyler's and her nightgown wasn't the new one she'd bought for company. At least she wasn't still nursing with her breast exposed.

His parents looked at her expectantly, so Mac made hasty introductions. "Mother, Dad, this is Megan Malone. My parents, Muriel and James Duncan."

Neither of them offered a hand to Megan. She had imagined Mac's parents as indulgent but intelligent, even bookish—his mother plump, his father stooped and absentminded—not these cool, sophisticated individuals who merely glanced at her assessingly before they turned back to their only son.

"We got your message," his mother said. "How's the child?"

"You have a grandson," Mac replied. "We've named him Tyler."

"Excellent," his father murmured, his expression more thoughtful than exuberant.

"Healthy?" his mother asked.

Mac glanced at Megan. "Yes, except for a slight case of jaundice the pediatrician assures us won't be a problem. Would you like to see him?'' The pride in his voice nearly brought tears to Megan's eyes.

His parents exchanged a look. ''In a moment,'' his mother said. ''First we'd like to talk to you.'' She gave Megan a tight smile. ''Alone, if you don't mind.''

Or even if she did, Megan figured. ''Of course,'' she replied, lifting the covers. ''Would you like me to leave?''

His mother's eyebrows shot up. ''No, of course not. We'll just step outside.''

Mac's neck had turned red, making Megan feel horrid for embarrassing him. ''We'll be right back.'' Almost defiantly, he leaned down and kissed her cheek. ''Do you need anything?''

Megan patted his hand. ''No, thanks. I'm fine.'' In truth, she was exhausted. It had been a long day, but there were too many emotions running around inside her like hamsters on a treadmill for her to relax. The first was worry about their son's health, even though Claire had insisted he'd be fine.

Mac's parents were a shock, as was his obvious discomfort around them. Perhaps he was just tired, or nervous about their reaction to Megan. Now that she had met them, she wondered if his childhood might not have been as rosy as she had painted it in her mind.

No sooner had the three of them filed out of the room than the door swung open again, revealing a familiar woman with long black hair and bright-blue eyes.

"Wendy!" Megan exclaimed, sitting up straighter as her cousin walked into the room. "What are you doing here?"

As Mac trooped after his parents, he glanced over his shoulder curiously at the woman entering Megan's room with a bouquet of flowers. Had she reached one of her friends after all?

His father led the way to an empty lounge with several overstuffed chairs in conversational group-ings and a TV playing a talk show without sound.

"Sit down," he said, making Mac feel as though he'd been pulled back through a time warp. Decid-ing that a protest wasn't worth the effort, he com-plied. His mother sat next to him, crossing one leg over the other as his father faced him, hitching up the fabric of his slacks with a practiced gesture.

Mac braced himself, assuming they were about to voice a complaint about his present situation. Their arrival on top of the emotional rush of watch-ing his son being born and his concern for the boy's jaundice was a hell of a lot to deal with. He needed a caffeine jolt and a few hours of sleep, not an inquisition.

"What are your plans?" his father asked, push-ing his glasses up on his nose in a familiar gesture. His intense gaze had always made Mac squirm with the knowledge that he would never measure up.

"Plans?" he echoed, refusing to be intimidated.

"Your plans for the future," his mother said.
"We want to make sure you're going to do the right
thing and marry this girl. Your son is a Duncan and
you need to legitimize your claim, or you'll find
you have precious little control over his future."

"These days even an unmarried father has
rights," Mac pointed out. As usual they were telling
him what he should do. Years ago he might have
gone against his own instincts rather than give them
the satisfaction of appearing to comply with their
wishes. He'd like to think he had outgrown that
streak of immature rebellion.

Now he got to his feet as his father's head
snapped back. "If Megan will have me, I intend to
marry her," Mac announced, voicing the idea that
had been taking shape in his mind since Tyler's
arrival. For a number of reasons it certainly made
sense on a practical level.

His parents both stood up. "That's great news,
son," his father said heartily, shaking Mac's hand
with more than his usual enthusiasm.

"I'm glad you've decided to be sensible," his
mother added, as if the credit for his decision be-
longed with her. "Better late than never. Under the
circumstances, you'll want to act quickly, of course,
but there's no reason for anyone back home to
know the exact dates."

She was thinking of their friends, Mac realized.
Having a baby out of wedlock fell below the Duncan standard.

"I'm sure no one cares," he offered.

She sniffed. ''Despite what you think, appearances are still important to people who matter. We have a position to maintain. Tyler is our grandchild, and we want to acknowledge him as such.'' Her expression didn't soften. ''You'd be making things extremely awkward for us if you and Margaret weren't married.''

''Her name is Megan,'' Mac said.

''Of course. Does she have family nearby?''

Mac shook his head.

''It's just as well. Under the circumstances, I'm sure you'll want to keep the wedding small.''

''That's up to Megan.'' As far as Mac was concerned, a simple ceremony before they left the hospital would be fine. ''I'll be sure to keep you posted.''

Except for a slight tightness around her mouth, his mother didn't betray any reaction to his failure to fall in with her wishes. For once Mac didn't even give a damn. He'd provided them with a grandson, which was what they wanted.

''I'm sure there's no need for your father and me to drive all the way back down here.''

Mac inclined his head. ''Of course not.'' Apparently it didn't occur to her that he might like having them present at his nuptials, and he wasn't about to suggest it.

''You'll let us know if you need anything?'' his father asked.

''Sure thing.''

After an uncomfortable pause he made no attempt to fill, his mother pleaded the start of a headache.

"Please make our excuses to Megan," she said as the three of them stood up and faced each other awkwardly. "It's getting late and we both have morning classes."

"Thanks for coming." He was surprised they'd bothered. It was only after he'd walked them to the elevator and watched the doors close, his relief at their departure making him feel both guilty and sad, that he realized they hadn't even remembered to go by the nursery and see his son.

"I'd love to stay and visit, but I promised Bud I wouldn't be long," Wendy said as she made a face at her watch and got to her feet. "He doesn't like me running around loose at night. He would have come with me if the other pharmacist hadn't been sick." She tucked her purse under her arm. "I'm glad you liked the blanket."

"I love the blanket," Megan corrected her. "Tyler's going home wrapped in it."

Wendy looked extremely pleased.

"Thanks for the flowers, too." Megan glanced at the bunch of implausibly bright blue carnations her cousin had brought. "Be sure to stop by the nursery on your way out."

"Wouldn't miss it," Wendy replied with a smile as she flipped back her hair. "You didn't think I drove all the way from Reno just to see you?"

Once a remark like that would have hurt unbearably. Now Megan knew better. She'd enjoyed her cousin's visit and listened with real interest to the snippets of family gossip Wendy brought with her. If Megan hadn't been so determined not to risk rejection at Aunt Ruth's funeral, she might have found out then that Wendy had changed since their childhood. Gone was the aloof older girl who resented sharing her room—and her mother—with a mere child. In her place was a nice woman Megan might one day count as a friend.

"Thank you for coming," she said quietly. "I did hope you could meet Mac before you left."

As if in response to her spoken wish, the door opened and he appeared. Megan was worried that he might be upset over whatever his parents had wanted, but he was smiling when he walked into the room.

As soon as she saw him, her heart gave a little leap of excitement. Despite his scruffy appearance, he was still the most attractive man she knew. Proudly she introduced him to Wendy.

"It's nice to meet someone from Megan's family," he said as he shook her cousin's hand. "Megan showed me the blanket you sent. It's lovely."

Color swept into Wendy's fair cheeks as she responded to his smile. He really was a hunk, Megan thought as she watched him charm the other woman without visible effort, and a nice hunk, too.

"This one's a keeper," Wendy pronounced when he finally released her hand. "Do you feel up to walking down to the nursery and showing me your son before I go?'' she asked Megan.

Mac held out her robe while she got out of bed. After she had slipped it on, his hands seemed to linger on her shoulders. Perhaps he was only making sure she was steady on her feet.

The three of them went slowly down the hall. She was dying to know what Mac's parents had wanted, and curious whether he'd tell her. Since their baby's birth, she felt a bond with him that went far deeper than romantic attraction. From the warmth in his dark eyes when he looked at her, he'd felt the change between them as well.

''What did your folks think of their first grandchild?'' she asked when he remained silent.

An unreadable expression crossed his face, gone again before she could interpret it. ''Oh, they've already embraced him into the Duncan clan,'' he replied after a barely perceivable pause.

Megan didn't know quite how to take his answer. ''I hope the jaundice didn't alarm them,'' she persisted, stopping for a moment to catch her breath. ''Did you tell them that Dr. Davis said there was no cause to be concerned?''

Mac stopped in front of the window to the nursery. ''Don't worry. They sure didn't seem worried about the jaundice when they left.''

''Which one is he?'' Wendy asked eagerly.

Megan spotted him in the second row and pointed him out proudly. He was sleeping beneath the healing lights, his little gnome face scrunched up into a frown that made her wonder what he was dreaming about.

"What a doll," Wendy said. "It's so hard to believe that my kids were that tiny when they were born."

Mac put his arm around Megan's waist. "He's a great kid," he said softly. "I know already he's going to do the Duncan clan proud."

Wendy's gaze sparkled with humor. "Takes after his dad," she teased with a wink at Megan.

Megan rested her head on Mac's shoulder and gazed through the glass. Motherhood was a challenge she was eager to face. The two things she needed for life to be perfect, she realized, were for Tyler to recover from the jaundice and for Mac to fall in love with her, just as surely as she had tumbled into love with him.

When Megan woke up early the next morning, Mac was already sitting in the chair holding Tyler. On the windowsill was a big bouquet of white roses and baby's breath in a crystal vase.

He hadn't gone home the night before until after Megan was settled into bed, and he'd promised to check on Cassius on the way. It had been beyond Megan's acting ability to say anything more about his parents than it was nice they had come by.

"How long have you been here?" she asked him now as she sat up and smothered a yawn with her hand. The nurses had waked her twice in the night to nurse the baby, but she didn't care how often they disturbed her if frequent feedings would help lower his TSB count and prevent the necessity for a transfusion.

Mac was leaning down to make faces at Tyler, but at Megan's question, he lifted his head and smiled. "I got here a few minutes ago, but I persuaded the nurse not to wake you until this little guy demanded breakfast. Did you get much sleep?"

"Enough," she replied. Knowing that he'd been watching her while she slept made her feel vulnerable, which was ridiculous after the intimacies they'd recently shared. "How about you?"

He'd changed into a white dress shirt, open at the neck, and dark slacks. "All I need is a few hours," he said, lifting Tyler up to plant a noisy kiss on his cheek. "Cassius sends his love."

"I'll bet. Thanks for taking care of him for me, and thank you for the roses. They're lovely," Megan said. On her way to the bathroom, she stopped to greet Tyler, resting her hand on Mac's shoulder and inhaling his scent, something spicy and understated.

When she came back out of the bathroom, he was still talking nonsense with a total lack of self-consciousness. The baby began to fuss and Mac looked up helplessly. "I'm still learning," he said with a hint of desperation in his voice.

"You're doing very well." Megan took Tyler and settled back into bed. As soon as she offered him her breast, he quieted down. While he nursed, Mac went to the window and looked out, hands in his pockets, apparently content to study the view from the second floor.

Megan wondered what he was thinking, but she didn't want to pry. "Would you watch him while I shower, or do you have to get to work?" she asked instead, once Tyler was satisfied.

Mac turned and took him from her. "Go ahead with your shower. We'll be fine. I wanted to be here when Dr. Davis came around, anyway. Elaine, my office manager, is dying to visit, but I held her off until this afternoon."

"Jill won't be back from her camping trip until tomorrow, but I'll call Patty later, and my neighbor, Blanche," Megan said as she gathered up her shower supplies and a clean nightgown. Part of her hated to leave them, even for a few minutes. "I'll be right back."

When she returned, feeling much better, breakfast trays were being delivered from a cart in the hallway and she realized she was starving.

Mac was sitting alone with a magazine in his lap.

"Where's Tyler?" she asked.

He closed the magazine and got to his feet. "One of the nurses took him down for his Phototherapy treatment. She promised to bring him back later."

As he continued to smile down at her, hands in the pockets of his slacks, Megan was glad she'd taken the extra time to dry her hair and apply a little makeup.

"Thank you again for the flowers." She laced her fingers together. What she wanted was to step into his arms, but she wasn't sure how he would react. If he rejected her, the awkwardness between them would be unbearable. For Tyler's sake, she had to put his relationship with his father ahead of her own wishes.

"There's something I wanted to discuss with you," Mac said.

Before Megan could reply, an attendant brought in her breakfast tray.

"Have you eaten?" Megan asked Mac.

"Yeah, earlier."

"Would you like some coffee?" the attendant asked him. "I can bring you some when I'm done with the trays."

"No, thanks."

He sounded impatient, arousing Megan's curiosity as she uncovered her breakfast dishes. "What did you want to talk about?" she asked after the attendant left.

"Go ahead and eat," he replied. "We'll talk afterwards." His expression was unreadable, but Megan's stomach knotted with concern.

"It sounds serious."

He shrugged, shifting from one foot to the other. "Maybe I'll run down to the cafeteria and get some coffee after all. Want anything else?"

Megan looked at the scrambled eggs, bacon, English muffin and fruit bowl. In order to feed Tyler, she had to consume a lot of calories. "I don't think so."

"Then I'll be right back."

As soon as he left, she attacked the food, more hungry than she realized. By the time he returned, she was nearly done. Taking the tray from her, he handed her an orange bag. Peanut butter M&M's!

"Dessert," he said.

"It seems like I'm always thanking you for something," Megan replied. "You're very thoughtful."

Looking uncomfortable with the compliment, Mac took a deep breath and sat down on the side of the bed.

"What did you want to talk about?" Megan put the candy aside for later. "Was it something your parents said?"

His brows bunched into a frown. "Why would you think that?" he demanded.

Stung by his tone, Megan shook her head. "No reason."

Outside the door, someone dropped a tray. It crashed loudly, followed by the sound of voices. As they faded, Mac surprised her by taking her free hand in his and smoothing his fingers over her knuckles.

"I know you wanted to raise Tyler alone," he began, head bowed as he continued to stroke her hand, "but I wondered if you'd had any second thoughts now that we've gotten to know each other better."

Fear gripped Megan, expanding in her chest until it ached from the pressure. Was Mac going after custody? Had he and his parents been scheming behind her back?

"What do you want?" she whispered through stiff lips as she yanked her hand free of his grasp. The idea of losing her baby was terrifying. Was she being unreasonable to want to keep him with her?

Megan looked away, biting her lip to keep the tears at bay. Was she going to lose her son as well as the man she'd begun to love?

"I can see from your expression that I'm handling this badly," Mac said hastily. "What I wanted to say is that there are a lot of reasons, practical reasons, for us to consider making our partnership more, uh, formal."

It took a moment for his words to sink in. Partnership? Had the miracle happened? Did Mac love her? "What are you suggesting?" she asked, unable to meet his gaze and plucking nervously at the sheet instead. Perhaps all he was suggesting was some kind of written contract.

He cleared his throat. "Now that we have a baby to consider, everything has changed." He sounded hoarse. "I never thought Tyler's birth would affect me this strongly." He hesitated. "I can't tell you how much I love that boy already."

Of course Megan was thrilled that he loved their son, but she wanted him to get to the part about his feelings for *her*. Curbing her impatience, she returned Mac's smile. "I know. I feel the same way about him. Isn't it amazing?"

"I care for you, too," Mac added belatedly.

Megan's hopes nose-dived. "Really?" she asked dryly. She'd never considered before how downright tepid to be cared for actually sounded, especially when you were desperately hoping for a declaration of undying love.

He took her hand again and leaned closer. "Legally it would simplify things," he said earnestly. "Financially it would make sense, and Tyler would have two parents to raise him together."

"*What* would make sense?" she demanded. The reasons he'd listed sounded more like a business proposal than anything remotely romantic. She remembered his words from before. He didn't believe in that kind of crap.

"I think we should get married," he said. "I have the big house and a good medical coverage. You can continue to work at home and watch him during the daytime. Yeah, marriage would be a practical solution."

"A solution to what?" Megan snapped. "I didn't realize there was a problem." The only problem was her broken heart, shattered into a thousand pieces. She could hardly breathe around the pain and disappointment piercing her as though she had turned into a giant pincushion.

Mac reared back as if her reaction had caught him by surprise. Maybe he expected her to fall into his arms and agree that marriage would be eminently practical. Megan felt more like screaming.

"I think you should leave now," she said instead, keeping her voice utterly calm. As calm as death, the death of a dream.

"I don't understand your reaction." Mac got to his feet. "Marriage is a good idea. I think we need to discuss it further."

Megan tipped her head back, willing the tears gathering behind her eyelids not to fall. "Was this what your parents wanted to discuss with you? Making your little bastard legitimate?" She could tell from his shocked expression that she'd guessed right.

"What they said doesn't matter. I was already thinking about proposing before they mentioned it."

"So they did bring it up?"

"Yeah, so what?" Apparently her lack of gratitude was beginning to annoy him. "They're concerned about Tyler's future, too. After all, he's a Duncan."

"Do you always try so hard to please your parents?" she demanded.

Color crept up his neck and his ears turned red. "Let's leave them out of this."

"I think you're the one who should leave," she insisted. If she didn't get some privacy soon, she was going to embarrass both of them by bursting into hysterical tears.

"Is that a no?" Mac asked.

"Damned right it is." She took refuge behind anger. Perhaps a healthy tantrum would keep the tears at bay until he was gone.

"I think you should take some more time," Mac said. "It's a big decision. I only brought it up now so you could think about it, although I'd figured we might get married right here in the hospital before you're released."

"Oh, that would be *practical,* wouldn't it?" she asked bitterly.

"It was just an idea." For a moment he stood looking down at her with a puzzled expression. Megan nearly relented, until he added, "It's for our son's sake that I suggested it."

Now tears did fill her eyes, tears of disappointment. "I grew up without love," she said angrily. "I won't raise my son without it, and I certainly won't consider marrying anyone without it. I appreciate what you're offering, and I can't begin to imagine what it cost you to ask, but I'm sorry. Marrying you is out of the question. When I take that step, it will be to enter a loving relationship and I cannot, will not, settle for anything less. I'd rather stay single for the rest of my life."

For a long moment after her speech, he was silent. "Well," he said, finally, "that's it, then. I guess I totally misread the situation." He bowed his head stiffly. "I'm sorry if I upset you."

"No, I'm sorry," she replied, her anger draining away as quickly as it had built, leaving her exhausted. "We have a son. Nothing will change that. I want to do what's best for him, and that means having you in his life. We'll work that out, okay?"

"Sure," he rasped.

Megan nearly felt sorry for him. For a moment he'd almost looked lost. Before she could think of anything to add, the door to her room swung open. In walked Claire, followed by Dennis Reid. They were both wearing white coats. At the sight of their expressions, Megan froze.

"Tyler!" she gasped, filled with icy panic. "Is he all right?"

Claire immediately came over and sat down on the edge of the bed. "Tyler is fine," she said firmly. "He's responding to the Phototherapy and his TSB is down."

Mac looked from her to Dennis Reid and back again. "Then what's the problem? Dennis, you look too pompous for me to think you just dropped by to offer your congratulations on the birth of my son."

Dennis and Claire exchanged glances. "That's the problem," Dennis replied, looking uncomfortable. "There's no easy way to say this, Mac. We typed the blood Dr. Davis drew from the baby in case there was a need for a transfusion." He drew in a breath. "I'm sorry, but the infant Ms. Malone gave birth to isn't your son."

Chapter Ten

Mac stared hard at Dennis, his blood rushing in his ears as he tried to make sense of what the chief of staff had just said.

"Of course Tyler's my son." Mac was vaguely aware of Megan gripping his hand tightly. Dr. Davis watched him with a worried frown. "Is this some kind of a bad joke?" Mac demanded.

"We have letters from the clinic," Megan stammered. "Mine's at home. I can show you." She turned to Mac with panic in her eyes. "Can you go over to my house and get it for me? It's on my desk in my office."

Dr. Davis eased her arm around Megan's waist. "Why don't you sit down. We already have a copy of that letter. It's not the problem."

Mac wanted to hit something. Dennis's jaw was a tempting target. Mac curled his hands into fists, but physical violence had never been his style. Besides, his legs were starting to shake with reaction. "Tyler must be my son," he protested. "He has my father's ears." How could a baby with Mac's father's ears not be a Duncan? None of this made any sense.

Dennis shook his head and clapped his hand on Mac's shoulder. "I'm sorry, buddy. The blood types don't match and of course there's no doubt that Ms. Malone is the mother."

"That's it!" Mac realized what must have happened. "The nursery accidentally switched the babies. It's happened before. Or the lab mixed up the blood samples." Part of him knew he was grabbing for straws, but he couldn't help himself.

Dennis was holding a file folder in his hand. "Believe me, Mac, the babies weren't switched. Apparently the problem started when the letter you wrote about your sperm sample was somehow mixed up with the paperwork for Ms. Malone's artificial donor and her class registration. Dr. Davis here was the one who originally ran it down, but the receptionist we suspect was responsible has quit and moved away, so we'll never know for sure. We've run some tests, though, and there's no question about the identity of Tyler's biological father."

"What's his name?" Megan asked. Her face was pale.

"I'm sorry, but the man was part of our donor

program. I've already talked to him and he insists on remaining anonymous,'' Dennis replied.

Sudden fury roared through Mac. ''I just lost a son and you're *sorry? That* doesn't cut it, Dr. Reid!''

Dennis ignored Mac's outburst. ''Rest assured the clinic will conduct an internal review,'' he told them both. ''As the chief of staff and as your friend, I can only say how much we deeply regret any pain this has caused either of you.'' He turned to Dr. Davis. ''Perhaps we'd better give them some time alone to absorb this?'' he suggested.

''In a minute,'' she replied firmly.

He pursed his lips and glanced down at his heavy gold watch. ''I have a luncheon appointment, but I should be in my office all afternoon.''

Neither Mac nor Megan said anything. Megan was perched on the edge of the bed, looking down at her hands, so Mac dropped into the chair and stared blankly out the window.

''Can I do anything?'' Dr. Davis asked.

''I don't think so.'' Megan's voice was flat.

Mac wondered whether she was relieved by this new development. The possibility that she might be was a painful one. ''Surely there's a possibility that you're wrong in this,'' he insisted to Claire.

''No, I'm sorry, but there isn't,'' she said with obvious regret. ''We located the original paperwork. Megan's donor was the one she requested. I wish I could give you different news, but everything checks out.''

"What about a DNA test?" Mac asked.

"Of course we can do one if that's what you want, but I can tell you now it will take a while and the results will be the same."

Mac didn't know what else to say.

After another awkward moment, Claire excused herself and left. Mac was vaguely aware that Megan looked as stunned as he felt.

"I got what I wanted," she muttered bitterly. "Be careful what you wish for." Tears coursed down her cheeks as she looked at Mac. Her chin wobbled. "I'm sorry."

Everyone kept saying that. At least he'd been wrong about her being relieved by the news. He could barely stand to look at her through his own pain. He knew they had to talk, but he felt like the ground had just fallen away beneath his feet. At any moment one of the nurses could walk in with Tyler.

How was Mac supposed to feel about the baby now? And about Megan, the mother of someone else's child?

"I can't do this," he stammered, knowing he was acting like a coward but unable to stop himself. "I have to get to work."

"When will you be back?" Megan whispered.

"I don't know. Later, I guess." Mac wanted to take her into his arms and comfort her, to tell her it didn't matter and that everything would be all right, but he wasn't sure this situation would ever right itself. He'd wanted a child of his own. Was that so wrong? Barely looking at her, he bolted from the room.

Megan waited for hours for Mac to come back so they could deal with the situation together. She thought about calling Wendy, but was afraid if she did all she'd do was cry.

While Tyler nursed, she studied his tiny features, but his appearance hadn't changed any since she'd thought he was Mac's child. There were no answers to be found on his precious little face. Had she only seen the evidence that she wanted so desperately to be there?

Jill came by in the afternoon. Before Megan knew what was happening, the whole sad story poured out.

"What a mess!" Jill burst out. "Can you sue the clinic?"

"On what grounds?" Megan asked quietly. "I have my baby, fathered by the donor I chose. If anyone has grounds for a lawsuit, I'd say it was Mac."

"Do you think he will?" Jill asked in a calmer voice as she scooped Tyler from Megan's arms and sat in the chair to look him over.

"I don't know. I haven't talked to Mac since we found out about the mix-up." Megan hadn't told Jill or anyone else about his proposal. Since she hadn't come clean about her feelings for him, either, her friend couldn't be expected to understand the turmoil Megan was going through.

"Well," she said, bending over Tyler to make kissing noises, "I bet you're glad everything's cleared up and you can take this little guy home. When are they letting you out?"

"In the morning," Megan replied listlessly, hoping Mac would show up before then or she'd never get any rest tonight. Now part of her wished she had accepted his proposal and married him right away like he wanted. He was an honorable man. Once they had exchanged vows he wouldn't have deserted her because Tyler wasn't really his son.

"Do you need a ride home?" Jill offered. "I can get time off from work and pick you up if you do. I have an infant seat in my car."

Megan had to bite the inside of her cheek to keep the tears at bay. "I don't know," she admitted. "Can I call you later?" She had assumed that Mac would take them home, but that was before she'd turned down his proposal, before they'd found out he had no reason to give Megan or her baby another thought.

Oh, God! First she had reluctantly allowed Mac into her life and now she was terrified of losing him.

Maybe he just needed time to sort through his feelings, adjust his thinking, and then he'd be back to tell her that nothing had really changed. And maybe the extra weight Megan had gained would magically disappear by tomorrow and her boobs wouldn't droop.

Jill must have realized she wasn't in the mood

for company. "I've got to run a couple of errands," she said, kissing Tyler's cheek as she handed him back. "Let me know about the ride."

After she left, the nurse came in to take him for his Phototherapy session.

"Can you leave him with me for a little while longer?" Megan asked, cuddling him close. "He's sleepy and I'd like to hold him for a bit."

The nurse hesitated. "Sure, why not? I'll be back in a half hour or so."

Mac must have been waiting in the hall. As soon as the woman left, he came in. His hair was standing on end as if he'd run his fingers through it repeatedly, and there was a smudge on his white shirt. He stopped just inside the doorway and leaned against the jamb, hands stuffed into his pockets.

"Hi," he said, his gaze barely touching Megan before it slid away. "How are you doing?" He didn't even glance at Tyler, asleep in the crook of her arm.

A chill went through Megan at the disinterest in Mac's voice. The distance between them might as well have been a hundred feet instead of less than a dozen. "I'm okay. How about you?"

He straightened and shrugged his wide shoulders. "I didn't make it to the office."

"Where have you been?" she asked.

"I just drove around for a while."

"Did you call your parents?" Who would he turn to if he needed comfort? She couldn't picture him getting it from his undemonstrative mother or silent father. Justine, perhaps? Jealousy, as sharp as a fillet knife, stabbed Megan. As far as she knew, the other woman had already left for California and the selfish side of Megan was glad.

"No, I haven't called them yet. I have no idea what to say to them. They wanted a grandchild."

What mattered to Megan was that he was here. She knew he and Tyler had bonded. Maybe his feelings went deep enough that the baby's true parentage wouldn't matter. Maybe—

"I came to say goodbye." Mac's voice was rough.

"Oh." It seemed like all she had done since Dennis and Claire had come in was fight to keep from crying. Now she struggled against the newest wave of tears that threatened to overwhelm her. Damn, but she wouldn't give a fig who Tyler's father was, if it didn't mean losing Mac.

How could he walk away? Neither she nor Tyler had changed in the last few hours. Did blood and genes have to be so very important? Surely the bond they shared went beyond that.

"Would you like to hold Tyler?" she asked in a desperate bid for time.

He hesitated. "Sure. None of this is his fault." Carefully he took the baby from her, holding him like a bomb that might explode.

It's not my fault, either, Megan wanted to shout. Instead she watched him stare at the son she'd believed they made together, and her heart quietly broke for the loneliness she saw etched on Mac's face.

For a man who professed not to believe in love, he was in desperate need of it, she realized. She wanted to beg him to stay in their lives, but it was already too late. She'd made her choice and now he had made his.

Mac handed Tyler back to her. He looked tired. "If you need anything," he began, and then he fell silent. They both knew she wouldn't call on him. "Well, good luck to both of you." Before Megan could speak, Mac turned on his heel and left the room. When Tyler started to fuss, Megan cried right along with him.

Outside in the hallway, Mac braced himself against the wall, head thrown back, eyes squeezed shut. His heart was thudding so hard he was afraid she would hear it from inside the room. His stomach was twisted into a knot of pain and his hands were curled into impotent fists. He felt as though there was a gaping hole where his heart had been.

This must be a little like what a parent who lost a baby felt. The shock, the wrenching loss, the stunned confusion. Mac had been able to keep it buried inside until he'd held Tyler's tiny body in his hands. Then it came crashing down like a tidal wave.

Megan refused to marry without love, and now Mac had lost the one tie that bound them together. If his son had never even existed, why did Mac feel so bereft?

From inside the room he could hear the baby's crying. Megan was singing a lullaby and Mac imagined her rocking Tyler in an effort to comfort him.

Who would console Mac? He couldn't think of anyone. For a moment he dropped his guard. His vision blurred and he dragged in a ragged breath. From down the hall the elevator bell pinged softly to signal its arrival on the maternity floor. The sounds of voices and footsteps grew louder. Pulling himself together, Mac wiped his hand over his face, glanced back with mingled longing and regret at Megan's door and strode purposefully down the hallway.

"Do you want me to stay for a little while?" Jill asked after she set Megan's tote on the couch and took the bag of groceries to the kitchen. "I don't have to be back to work until after lunch, if you'd like me to fix something here."

Megan sank into a chair, clinging to Tyler. This wasn't at all the way she'd pictured their homecoming, but she had to stop thinking about might-have-beens. Mac had made it clear he was out of their lives for good.

"If you don't mind, I'd rather just get the baby settled in, become reacquainted with my cat and take a nap," she told Jill apologetically. "Thanks so much for the ride, though, and for stopping at the store. I really appreciate everything."

Jill put the perishables in the refrigerator and came back into the living room. "This was in the kitchen.'' She held up the spare key Megan had given to Mac so he could feed Cassius. He must have left it last night.

''Just put it on the counter,'' she told Jill.

If her friend was curious, she didn't let on. ''Is there anything else you need?'' she asked instead.

''I can't think of anything,'' Megan replied. Bring Mac back to us, her heart cried before she determinedly shut out the silent plea. Mac was in her past, albeit the very recent past, but it was the future and her baby that needed Megan's full attention now. No regrets, no looking back.

Before she'd left the hospital, Claire had come by to tell her Tyler's bilirubin level had dropped into the normal range and he was ready to go home.

''Please call me,'' she'd insisted, pressing her card into Megan's hand. ''My home number is on the back. Maybe we can have a cup of coffee or lunch after you've gotten settled.''

Thinking about it, Megan had no idea what she'd said in reply, but she knew from the childbirth classes that Claire was a compassionate woman as well as a competent doctor. She would have understood Megan's distraction.

Jill, too, extracted a promise from Megan that she would call if she needed anything at all. ''I'll see you soon,'' she said. ''Enjoy that precious little bundle you brought home with you.'' With a last waggle of her fingers, she left, shutting the front door behind her.

As soon as Jill was gone, Cassius meowed from

the top of the stairs. With a cat's instinct, he knew that something in his world was different.

Megan called to him and he made his way carefully down to where she sat. She stroked his head and murmured to him while he purred and butted her hand. When he jumped up onto the couch, Tyler stirred in his blanket.

For a moment, Cassius froze, whiskers quivering. Every muscle was poised for flight, yet curiosity kept him enthralled. While Megan watched carefully, he investigated the bundle that wiggled and made noise. After a minute, the cat lost interest and hopped down.

After Megan fed him and dealt with his litter box, she washed her hands at the kitchen sink and played her messages. Patty had called, still sick, Blanche, an editor, someone trying to sell her aluminum siding and one offering to switch her long distance carrier.

There was no message from Mac, but she hadn't expected him to call.

Resolutely Megan went into the living room and picked up her baby. "Let's show you your new digs," she suggested.

As usual, he seemed to respond to her voice. She would have sworn that he smiled, but she knew from what she'd learned in class that it was probably only gas. Soon, though, his personality would start to emerge. She would be the most important person in the world to him, just as he already was to her.

Cradling him carefully, she went up the stairs to his nursery. As unconventional as they might seem to some people, together she and Tyler were now the family that Megan had always dreamed about.

She walked through the doorway to the nursery and froze. The room was exactly as she had left it, right down to the mobile over the crib, with one large exception. A bentwood rocker with a big blue bow and a yellow checkered pad sat by the window, its flowing curves gleaming softly in the light.

There was no tag, no note, but Megan knew that Mac was the only one who could have left the rocker here. He must have brought it when he fed the cat.

Megan ran her free hand over the polished wood of the arm as she admired the intricate design of the back. The rocker was the ideal place for her to sit with Tyler. Surprising her with it was the kind of gesture she had come to expect from Mac.

Thanking him for the extravagant gift gave her the perfect reason to call. As soon as she had fed Tyler and put him down in the crib, she went to the phone in her office.

Elaine answered on the second ring.

"It's Megan Malone," she said, throat tightening against a sudden attack of nerves. Maybe she should have planned better what to say. She only had one shot, but it was too late now to go back. "Is Mac there?"

"Oh, Megan," Elaine exclaimed, her warm voice reaching through the phone like a pat on the head. "How are you and the baby doing? I'm so sorry I didn't make it over to see you, but things have been crazy here."

And you lost your reason to visit Tyler, Megan wanted to add. "We're fine," she said instead. "We just got home a little while ago. May I speak to Mac? I know he must be busy, but I promise not to keep him long."

"I'm sorry, dear, but he's not here."

That was odd. It was midmorning and he'd already missed a lot of time. "He's not sick, is he?" Megan's hand tightened on the phone. Mac was so strong, so solid, that she couldn't imagine him ill or unable to cope with life's little glitches in any way.

"No, he left for Dallas first thing this morning. It was very sudden. I didn't know he was going until late last night. I guess there was a problem with one of the playhouses we did for an oil company executive." She chuckled. "Well, I guess you wouldn't call it a problem. The man's added a wing to the main house, and he wants the playhouse to match. He's been trying to get Mac to come down for a month."

Megan was stunned. "When will he be back?"

"Not for a week. He's going straight from Dallas to a big home show in New Orleans. Is there something I can do? Do you want me to try to reach him for you?"

How much did Elaine know? Megan noticed that she didn't ask if it was an emergency, didn't offer to give Megan the number at his hotel. Mac had never mentioned going to Dallas and he'd talked about sending someone else to New Orleans in his place.

"No, don't bother," she told Elaine. "It's nothing that can't wait." After Megan hung up, she tiptoed into the nursery and checked on Tyler, who was sleeping peacefully. For a little while she stood beside his crib and listened to his tiny snores, wanting to touch him so badly that she ached with it.

Back at her desk, she took some note paper from the drawer and wrote Mac a polite note. Maybe his being gone was for the best. Other than thanking him for the rocker, what more was there left to say between them that hadn't already been said?

Mac let his hand holding the video camera drop to his side and wiped the perspiration from his face with his bandanna handkerchief. It was hot in Dallas, and humid as a swamp, but Ben Carter was a valued customer who had recommended Small World to several of his friends.

In front of Mac was the main house of the Carter estate, a vision in mellow red brick and glass. The architect had done such a good job with the new addition that Mac wouldn't have been able to tell it from the original structure if he didn't know where to look.

"I found the blueprints," Ben called to him from the front entrance, waving a roll of paper. "Do you have what you need yet? Jennifer's making juleps. Come and join us by the pool.''

Mac figured he had enough footage of the addition to replicate it when he got back to Buttonwood. He'd already shot the side and back elevations. The blueprints would help with the scale. The video would show the details of the exterior.

''I'm done,'' he called back. ''A cold drink sounds great.''

Ben waited in front of the massive double doors while Mac crossed the lawn. Together the two men walked through the spacious house to the patio area.

''Can we change your mind about staying with us for a couple of days?'' Ben asked. ''We're having a barbecue tomorrow night. It would be a chance for you to meet some people.'' He kissed his wife's cheek as she handed each of them a tall glass dripping with condensation. ''Our friends have kids and kids need places to play,'' he added with a grin.

Mac thanked Jennifer for the drink and took a long swallow. He was tempted to accept the invitation until he noticed a black-haired woman walking toward them. With her was the little girl Mac had built the playhouse for and in the woman's arms was a baby.

''Hi, Cory!'' Jennifer exclaimed as the little girl, blonde like her mother, let go of the nanny's hand and ran over to her. ''Did you have a good nap?''

''Hi, Mommy. Hi, Daddy. Hi, Mac.'' She hugged Jennifer's legs for a moment as Mac returned her boisterous greeting and then Ben swung her effortlessly onto his shoulders as she shrieked in mock alarm.

Mac went tense all over as the nanny handed the baby to Jennifer. He had dark hair like his father and he was bigger than Tyler, but the sight of the happy little family squeezed Mac's chest so tight he thought he'd pass out.

"I want you to meet Ben Junior," his host said proudly as Jennifer dismissed the nanny and cuddled the baby to her curvaceous bosom.

"That's my brother," Cory exclaimed from her perch on her daddy's shoulders. "All he does is sleep and eat. Maria says he'll play with me when he's older."

"That's all you did when you were his size," her mother reminded her, reaching up to tweak a golden curl. "Someday Benjy will be big like you."

"I'm sorry I can't stay for the barbecue," Mac blurted. "I've got an appointment in New Orleans."

Both the Carters expressed their disappointment and then Jennifer excused herself to take both children back inside and check on the dinner preparations. Mac hoped Ben hadn't noticed his apparent lack of interest in his new son, but he couldn't have held that child in his arms if this deal, or his life, had depended on it.

"In fact," he added as he finished the julep, "I'd better get back to the hotel. I left some papers there that I need in order to discuss some business with another client I promised I'd call this evening."

"Consuela's fixing tacos," Ben replied. "Sure you can't stay and eat?"

Mac was tempted. If lunch was any indication, their cook beat hotel food without question. He wondered if the kids would join them, but there was no way he could ask. Watching the family interact in the way he'd pictured doing with Megan and Tyler was more than he wanted to deal with. It was too damned soon.

"Let me take a rain check," he told Ben.

"Okay, but you know how much it rains here. And the next time you come down, I'm fixing you up with my cousin. It's time you settled down and started a family of your own."

Long after Mac had gotten back to the hotel and gone up to his room, Ben's words still circled in his mind like vultures waiting to pick at his carcass. More than once he reached for the telephone only to stop himself at the last moment.

Were Megan and Tyler safely home? Had she gotten a ride with one of her friends? He should have asked Elaine to make sure she did, but he'd left town in such a hurry this morning that he hadn't thought about it. All he'd wanted to do was to put some miles between them in the vain hope of keeping the images at bay—images of Megan and the baby Mac no longer had the right to love.

Tyler wasn't his, there was no blood bond, so why didn't the feelings go away?

Did Megan like the rocking chair? Was Tyler over the jaundice? Once again he toyed with the idea of calling, but his courage failed when he realized how awkward the conversation would be.

She didn't have feelings for him. Tyler wasn't his. Mac had no right to either of them and no way to find what Ben had. Maybe if Mac said the words enough, they'd eventually sink in and he could move on.

He picked up the television remote and flipped through the channels, but nothing held his interest. He considered going back downstairs to the bar. Perhaps feminine companionship would distract him. He pictured Megan, ripely pregnant and sexy as sin, and swore under his breath. Another woman wasn't the answer. He glanced at the bed, but he wasn't sleepy. With a muttered curse, he turned to the small hospitality bar instead.

Chapter Eleven

"I know it's a cliché, but he's growing so fast." Claire Davis had called Megan to suggest they meet for lunch at Mom & Pop's, a local diner that had been in Buttonwood for years.

"He's wonderful," Megan agreed, looking down at her rapidly growing son with a smile. "I don't know what I'd do without him." The two of them had settled into a comfortable routine and she was learning to take each day as it came.

"I don't mean to pry," Claire said hesitantly after a few moments of idle conversation, "but have you seen Mac Duncan at all?"

Megan shook her head, relieved that the tears she'd grown used to battling didn't come. "Not since I left the hospital. Have you?"

Claire took a drink of her diet cola. "He called my office once to ask how Tyler was doing. Of course I couldn't discuss anything specific with him, but I was able to reassure him in general terms that Tyler's in good health. I hope that was all right. At the time I suggested he contact you, but obviously he didn't heed my advice. I'm sorry. I can only guess how traumatic this situation has been for both of you."

Megan was surprised he'd called Claire. Did it hurt him to be shut out, or was distance what he wanted? From the way he had dropped out of her life, it certainly seemed to be. There had been no response to her note thanking him for the rocking chair and she had no further reason to contact him. No reason she'd admit.

"I'm glad you invited us to lunch," she told Claire after they'd given their orders to the waitress. A change of subject seemed like a good idea. "I was turning into a recluse, so it's great to get out and talk to another adult."

"Over and over I've witnessed how easy it is to become isolated, especially when you don't work outside the home," Claire agreed. "I remind my classes that stimulation and new experiences are good for babies, but they're also a necessity for new moms. I—"

"Oh, let me see the little precious," gushed another voice. Millie Johnson, the owner of the diner, leaned over Tyler as she wiped her hands on her apron. "What a doll." She greeted Claire and Megan warmly. "I would have come over sooner, but there was a crisis in the kitchen. How are you both? Megan, you're looking good for a new mother."

"Thanks. I'm doing great." Maybe if she said it often enough, it would come true. Physically she was doing well. It felt good to get back into her regular clothes and not waddle when she walked. Perhaps she'd do better to count her blessings, the primary one being her healthy son, rather than pine for a man who didn't want either of them.

"May I?" Millie asked, reaching for Tyler.

"Of course." Megan watched anxiously as the older woman scooped him up and tucked him into the crook of her arm as easily as she might a sack of flour. Jabbering nonsense as he stared up at her, she carried him away, stopping at every booth and stool in the small diner to show him off as if she'd given birth herself.

"Millie needs a family of her own," Claire observed as they disappeared into the kitchen. "It's obvious she's a frustrated mother hen."

Megan could hear Millie's booming voice over the rattle of dishes. "She's not married?" Millie had been one of the first people Megan met when she came to Buttonwood, but she only knew the restaurateur from her infrequent visits to the diner.

Claire shook her head. "Millie's parents opened this place years ago. From what I hear, she started waitressing when she was still a kid. Since Millie took over, I think she's been here twenty-four hours a day."

The subject of their conversation returned with Tyler as the waitress brought their plates. When he was tucked safely back into his carrier, munching on his fist, the phone by the register rang and Millie excused herself.

Claire eyed Megan's burger and fries with a covetous expression as she poked at her salad with her fork. "If I ate like that, I'd gain five pounds."

"I'm enjoying it while I can," Megan replied. "Once I stop nursing, I'll be eating salads, too."

For a few moments they enjoyed their meals in silence as Tyler babbled to himself and kicked his tiny feet in their blue booties.

"What's new at the clinic?" Megan asked idly, nibbling on a fry. "Any juicy scandals?"

As she halved a tomato wedge, Claire frowned thoughtfully. "You met Rachel Arquette, didn't you? She's a nurse—dark-haired, gorgeous?"

"We met. Is she still seeing Dennis Reid?"

Claire rolled her eyes. "There's an odd couple if I ever saw one, and I don't mean just the age difference. I don't get the attraction, at least not on *her* part. Well, our Rachel is—to use the expression—with child, but she's not saying who's responsible."

"Isn't Dennis the father?" Megan asked. "He was acting pretty possessive when I met them." She didn't normally indulge in gossip, but listening to Claire was a pleasant distraction from the unresolved issues in her own life, albeit a temporary one.

"No one knows and Rachel's not saying," Claire replied, leaning closer. "She was seeing another doctor for a while, a real dreamboat named Colt Rollins. We all thought they were serious."

"What happened?" Megan asked.

"Colt up and left town very suddenly. Here's the interesting part." Glancing around, she lowered her voice. "It was Dr. Reid who sent him to New Mexico on temporary assignment. Some people think he did it to give himself a chance to get next to Rachel."

"So this other doctor could be the father?" Megan asked, struggling to keep all the players straight.

"That's what we're all wondering. I'm sure Dennis would like to take the credit, but there's another rumor that she might have gotten involved with Hank Miller from the sheriff's department, after Colt and before Dennis. Do you know Hank?"

Megan shook her head. "I try to stay out of trouble with the law."

"Funny," Claire drawled. "Well, Hank's a big flirt, but he can be pretty close-mouthed when it comes to his private life. Jessica Wilson, the administrative assistant at the clinic, actually had the nerve to ask him about Rachel, but he just laughed and took the fifth, so no one knows whether the two of them actually got together or not."

Claire sat back in her seat. "Heavens, you'll think all we do at the clinic is gossip and speculate about everyone else."

Megan grinned. ''Don't you?''

''Not the patients,'' Claire said in a serious tone. ''Only the staff is fair game.''

Megan adjusted the blanket around Tyler as he yawned and his eyelids fluttered. Maybe he'd sleep for a little while. Her breasts felt full, but she wanted to wait until she got home to feed him. ''Sounds like Nurse Arquette gets around.''

''Well, Hank Miller is only speculation,'' Claire admitted, stealing one of Megan's fries, ''and Dennis is strutting around like a prize bull in a cow herd, but I really thought Rachel cared for Colt.'' She shook her head. ''There's no accounting for love, I guess.''

''What about you?'' Megan asked.

Claire's smile was wary. ''What about me?''

Megan shrugged. Perhaps she was prying into something Claire didn't feel comfortable answering. ''Anyone special in your life?''

The other woman sighed and tossed her auburn hair. ''I wish, but who has time for romance?''

''Not me, that's for sure,'' Megan replied dryly as Tyler stirred. His eyes popped open and he began to fuss. She picked him up and tried to comfort him while Claire signaled for the check. He wasn't about to be satisfied with words, though, his crying escalating in both volume and frequency.

''I'll pay for this and meet you outside,'' Claire said as Megan jiggled Tyler without success. ''I've got to get back to work anyway.''

''Let me give you some money.''

"Next time." She pulled out her wallet, grabbed Megan's diaper bag and headed for the register.

A few minutes later, after Megan had thanked her for lunch and promised to stay in touch, they parted company. Claire went back to the clinic and Megan headed home with Tyler in his car seat. For some reason he stopped crying as abruptly as he'd started, filling the car with blessed silence.

As she drove down the main street, she spotted Mac's pickup in front of the hardware store. The cab was empty and so was the sidewalk. Megan was tempted to circle the block and park down the street in the hopes of catching a glimpse of him. She had actually slowed to make the turn when she realized how pathetic she was being.

"Get a life," she muttered under her breath as she accelerated through the intersection, but her heart was hammering and her breathing was strained. She missed him, missed being able to share Tyler's daily accomplishments and her own concerns. Most of all, she regretted never knowing where her relationship with Mac might have gone, given time and opportunity.

At her checkup a few days before, Dr. Gould had given her permission to "renew her regular activities." The sight of Mac's truck and the memory of the kiss they'd shared made her long to explore one or two of those regular activities with him.

From the back seat, Tyler began to cry. As Megan turned onto her street, she wanted to throw back her head and howl right along with him.

*   *   *

It had been well over a month since Mac's world had tilted on its axis and he had lost both Megan and Tyler. A week after his parents had visited the hospital, an elaborately wrapped baby gift had come to Mac's house. Inside was an engraved silver mug similar to the one he'd had as a child. Last he'd noticed, his was displayed in the antique china cabinet in his parents' dining room, on the same shelf as the silver tea set they'd been given by the president of the university for their twenty-fifth anniversary.

Tyler Duncan was engraved on the new cup in ornate lettering. His mother's lack of subtlety made Mac shake his head before he shoved the cup in a drawer beneath some towels so he wouldn't have to look at it. Under the circumstances he didn't think Megan would appreciate the cup with the Duncan name on it. He knew his mother had been ticked off at the time by his failure to respond to her messages inquiring about his marriage plans, but he just hadn't been ready to explain.

This morning Mac had driven to Denver to visit his parents, who had a day off from their classes. They'd been surprised he was alone until he explained the reason for his visit. Now as he drove back through Buttonwood on his way home, it still amazed him how swiftly they had changed their tune concerning the baby who was no longer their dear grandson.

''It's fortunate that you didn't marry the woman

before the truth came out,'' his mother said with a sniff. ''At least there won't be any legal complications to deal with later on.''

''You make it sound as though Megan set the whole thing up to trap me,'' he replied, at a loss why he felt compelled to defend her without merely admitting she'd rejected his marriage proposal. ''She was as shocked by the turn of events as I was.''

His mother regarded him with a doubtful expression. His father, as usual, remained silent as he filled his pipe as precisely as if he were constructing a homemade bomb.

''Well, how could one expect a woman who was impregnated by a test tube to have any idea who had fathered her child?'' his mother said with a disdainful curl to her lip. ''The whole thing makes me shudder.''

''You weren't shuddering when you thought Tyler was a Duncan,'' Mac observed. ''Oh, I forgot, you didn't take the time to see him at the hospital, did you? Now you won't have to bother. Tyler *Duncan* no longer exists.''

''I don't understand why you're so upset,'' his mother replied. ''I would think you'd be relieved. If not for that blood test, you might have been saddled with another man's child.''

Perhaps it was the echo of his own fear that irritated Mac the most. ''Tyler is still the same child he was before I knew,'' he declared rashly. ''He's a great kid and I miss him. Every day I wonder about him." He didn't add that he missed Tyler's mother as well. That was too personal to present for his mother's clinical dissection.

Her eyebrows rose. "But you have absolutely no connection to him. How on earth can you say you miss a little boy who is nothing to you?"

Her question still rang in his ears as he drove by the city park and glanced over at the neat green square with its benches, its band pavilion and its statues of dead heroes. How could Mac have attempted to explain to his mother what he didn't himself understand?

Now his hands tightened on the wheel as he caught a glimpse of a slim woman with dark blonde hair pushing a stroller through the park. Even as he told himself it couldn't possibly be Megan, he was pulling over to the curb for a better look.

The sun was bright as Megan made her way down the sidewalk. Despite the canopy protecting Tyler from the rays, she was concerned that he'd get too warm. Before she could turn the stroller around and head for home, she looked up and saw Mac walking toward her.

Oh, my, but he looked good.

Legs trembling with sudden nerves, she stopped in her tracks. Her hands gripped the stroller handle so tight it might have squawked in protest if it had a voice. Despite her repeated attempts to forget MacGregor Duncan, she'd fantasized about running into him again—just not when she was wearing cut-off shorts and an old T-shirt, with straight hair and no makeup. In her imagination she was dressed in a slinky formal dress with a slit up the side. Her makeup was flawless, her perfume cost the earth and her heels were taller than her upswept hairdo.

Mac came to a halt about five feet away. "I nearly didn't recognize you," he said, smile crooked. "You've changed." His gaze traveled over her with stark male appreciation, making her grateful she'd lost most of the weight she'd gained with Tyler.

"You haven't," Megan breathed. In his charcoal slacks and pale-gray dress shirt with the sleeves rolled back, he was every bit as attractive as she remembered. When he continued to stare, she realized it was the first time he'd seen her in regular clothes.

"How have you been?" he asked, voice gravelly.

"Fine, and you?" It was all she could do to keep her hands off him, and this time she couldn't blame the magnetic pull on hormones.

"I've been out of town more than I like," he replied, "traveling on business."

"Lots of orders for playhouses?"

His sheepish grin deepened the grooves in his cheeks. "We've added a line of custom doghouses. They're selling so fast we've had to add another man. Now Elaine wants us to start building cat condos, too."

"That's wonderful." Megan's smile felt like paint that had dried. "Maybe I'll get one for Cassius someday."

"How's the baby?" He peered into the stroller where Tyler lay contentedly.

"Oh, Mac, he's wonderful," she burst out. "I adore him. Would you like to hold him?"

Naked longing flashed across his face and his hands flexed at his sides before a shutter slammed down, hiding his expression as though it had been wiped away. She knew he was going to refuse. Before he could, she picked Tyler up and closed the distance between them.

"See how much he's grown?"

With fingers that trembled, Mac touched the baby's cheek. "Hi, guy." His voice was gruff.

Tyler obliged by drooling and making a gurgling noise. For a long moment, Mac searched the baby's face below his little red sun hat as though he was memorizing the tiny features, but he made no move to take him. Finally Tyler began to fuss, so Megan put him back in his stroller.

"He's a good baby," she said.

Mac's gaze seared her. "And you're happy?"

A dozen replies crowded her tongue, but she rejected each of them. "We're getting there. How about you?" She wanted to run her hands over his shoulders, his chest, his hair, to see if he felt as good as she remembered. Then she realized his expression had changed, intensified.

"I've missed you." His voice was a rough whisper and there was a hot light in his eyes she'd never seen before. "You look so good."

The air around Megan, already warm, turned sultry. She had never felt so vulnerable. ''I think about you sometimes.'' Talk about understatement!

His gaze dropped to her mouth and lingered there, like an elusive caress she could almost taste.

''I'm glad.''

''Would you like to come home with us?'' she blurted.

His eyes widened in obvious surprise and he took a step back. ''Excuse me?''

''I only meant that I made some lemonade,'' she stammered. ''It's a warm day. You might be thirsty.'' She couldn't stop looking at his mouth, the shape, the fullness, and remembering the way it felt when he'd kissed her.

She was playing with fire, teasing them both, but it was too late to retract the invitation. Too late to squelch the feelings rising inside her like lava bubbling up from an active volcano. Perhaps he'd have the good sense to say no before they were both burned to a crisp.

''Sure,'' he said instead. ''Something wet and tart sounds good right now.''

The air seemed to crackle between them. ''Did you bring your truck?'' she asked. ''We can meet you at the house.'' She wondered why he would bother coming to the park when he had such a lovely yard of his own.

He gestured toward the street. ''I parked over there somewhere. It's only a couple of blocks to your place. As long as you don't mind holding Tyler, you can ride with me.''

He must have taken Megan's hesitation as concern that he didn't have a car seat. "I'll drive very carefully," he added.

She couldn't help herself. She wasn't yet ready to let him go. "Okay."

Circling the stroller, Mac began pushing it in the direction from which he'd come as Megan walked along with him and restrained herself from skipping with excitement. Another couple coming toward them with two small children smiled and nodded as they passed.

They must have thought she and Mac were a couple, too, out with their new baby. We could have been a family, Megan thought, and her heart ached for lost opportunities.

Mac didn't speak until they reached the truck. "Hop in," he said, opening the passenger door. "I'll hand you the baby and put the stroller in the back."

She wondered if he felt anything when he picked Tyler up. If she was to find out that by some bizarre twist of fate he wasn't really her baby, would she stop loving him? Apparently Mac's feelings were easy to shut off, but he'd warned her that he didn't believe in love.

She should have listened.

Megan climbed into the cab and fastened her seat belt. After Mac had handed her the baby, he tucked her purse and the diaper bag at her feet. Then he collapsed the stroller, laid it in the truck bed and walked around to the driver's door.

When he got in behind the wheel, the roomy cab seemed suddenly crowded. The air was warm and he rolled down his window. "All set?" he asked, glancing at her as he started the engine.

Megan shifted Tyler in her arms. "We're fine." She wondered what Mac was thinking. He didn't speak again, but she caught him looking at her more than once. When their gazes met, he smiled.

It took all of Megan's control not to run her free hand over his bare forearm. His skin was tanned the color of warm oak and the light sprinkling of hair was sunbleached. Her fingers itched, her senses hummed and desire curled low in her stomach.

By the time she led the way through her front door, Tyler was asleep in her arms. Mac went with her when she put him in his crib and watched while she settled him in. With a tiny sigh, the baby went back to sleep. Sneaking out of the nursery, Megan left the door ajar so she could hear if he fussed.

When she and Mac got to the top of the stairs, he captured her arm with his hand.

"About that lemonade," he began, voice soft.

Disappointment hit Megan like water from a hose. He was going to make an excuse and leave. There was nothing here to hold him, even for a few more moments.

She folded her arms across her chest and pressed her lips together so he wouldn't see them tremble. Before she could speak, he cupped her chin in his hand and leaned down until his mouth hovered near hers.

"I'm not really thirsty. Are you?"

Chapter Twelve

Looking at Mac as his intention sank in, Megan couldn't breathe for the desire rising inside her like a huge hungry wave of pure longing. "What did you have in mind?" she asked when she finally found her voice.

To her dismay, he tipped back his head, eyes squeezed shut. His jaw was clenched and the cords in his neck stood out. "I dream about you." His voice was low and thick with desire that radiated from him, matching Megan's own. He shook his head. "I can't ask."

Just one time, she thought, for closure. "You don't have to ask."

He froze, looking at her through narrowed eyes. "Are you sure? Has the doctor—"

She nodded slowly, an hysterical bubble of laughter rising in her throat. "Normal activity," she murmured, unable to keep the smile from her lips. "If what you're looking for falls within those parameters, I'd say it's a go."

Initially her words puzzled him, but slowly realization dawned. Dusky color ran up his cheeks and his eyes glittered with stark hunger. A muscle jumped in his cheek. Then suddenly he turned his back, raking both hands through his hair as he swore softly. "I'm not prepared."

Megan remembered the item that had caused the most laughter and a good bit of shock at her baby shower. "I am."

"Really?" His brows arched.

Megan shrugged. "It's a long story, but I can tell it to you now if you'd like." Damn, but she was almost enjoying this. The anticipation stinging her like the bites from a thousand fire ants was mirrored on Mac's face.

"Hell, no," he growled. "Save it for later."

To her surprise, he didn't kiss her. Instead he scooped her into his arms. "Your bedroom?"

"Uh-huh." Blushing, she buried her face against his hard chest. He gave off heat like a wood stove. She rubbed her cheek against the front of his shirt, but before she could fumble with the button, he tossed her lightly onto her bed and followed her down.

The desire that had been simmering between them since she first spotted him in the park ex-

ploded like an action scene in a Stallone movie.
Mac braced himself above Megan and she cradled
his face in her hands as he leaned closer. Their legs
tangled as they came together in a scorching kiss.
He rocked against her, hard as iron, and his breath
expelled in a long hiss. She slid her hands down
the long, sleek muscles of his back, pulling him
closer yet.

The part of her brain still capable of rational
thought hoped that Tyler took a nice long nap. The
rest of her melted into Mac. He rolled, taking her
with him. Greed propelled them as they raced to
release buttons, undo belts, kick off shoes and free
zippers. Clothing was stripped away. Hands explored bare skin. Lips nibbled and tasted. Teeth
nipped. Megan sighed. Mac groaned.

"I've wanted—" he growled.

"My body..." Megan began apologetically,
wanting to hide herself.

"—is beautiful," he finished for her as they
rolled again. He propped himself up on his elbow,
his other hand stroking so tenderly she could have
wept. "I don't want to hurt you."

"Please," she whispered, arching like a bow, unable to wait as the fire raced through her. Need
clawed, heat burned. Paradise hovered just beyond
her reach. She plucked urgently at his shoulders.
"Now. I need you now."

He lingered until she sobbed. Then he sheathed
himself with clumsy fingers. "Are you sure?" he
gasped, poised over her.

She loved him for asking, nearly hated him for waiting. "Please, please, please."

He tried to be gentle, but she wouldn't have it. She yielded. He claimed her. They merged, coupled and mated, fingers linked, bodies joined. Then, wrapped together, gazes locked, they leaped into the fire.

The second time was as leisurely as the first was rushed, as smooth as the first was not. This time Mac's patience exceeded Megan's pleas. Slowly, sweetly, he slipped inside. This time they soared, and then they slept.

With a mother's ear, Megan was awakened by fussing from the nursery. Beside her, Mac slept on, as relaxed as a big cat in a patch of sunshine. His arm anchored her close. His deep, steady breathing ruffled her hair. She cuddled into his heat with a sigh of contentment, but she didn't want Tyler to wake him. Carefully, reluctantly, she eased out from under his arm, smiled at his expression of utter peace and padded naked to the nursery.

"It's okay, sweetie. Mama's here," she soothed in a sing-song voice as she lifted her baby and got him into a dry diaper. A few moments later she crawled back beneath the covers, humming softly, and fed her baby as her man slept on. She was nearly done when she realized that Mac's eyes were open and he was watching her.

"What are you doing?" he asked hoarsely as he sat up, rubbing one hand over his face.

''Isn't it obvious?'' Blotting Tyler's rosebud mouth with the corner of the sheet, she smiled contentedly. ''He woke up, so I brought him back here with us. Want to hold him?''

For a moment she though Mac would comply.

''Uh, no. That's okay.'' He swung his legs over the side of the bed, shoulders hunched. Despite the warmth of the afternoon, she felt a sudden chill. Was she pushing too hard?

''What's wrong?'' she asked. Maybe he was worried about crushing the baby.

His back was to her as he reached for his clothes. ''Nothing.'' He stood up to pull on his shorts and stepped into his slacks. While she watched, biting her lip, he shrugged into his wrinkled shirt.

''I'll put Tyler back in his crib,'' she offered, hurt that Mac was ignoring them both as he put on his socks and dug around for his shoes.

''I have to go.'' Face in profile, he shoved in his shirttail and buckled his belt.

She'd made a major mistake, she realized. He must feel threatened, or merely saddened by what he'd lost. Either way there were issues he hadn't yet dealt with.

Laying the baby down carefully, she grabbed her robe off the chair and slipped into it. ''What about that lemonade I promised?'' she couldn't keep herself from asking. ''I'll put Tyler in his swing.''

She'd gotten what she wanted, to know what his loving was like. So why did she feel so hollow?

Would she see Mac again or was this it? She

wanted to ask, but knew she'd sound grasping and desperate. That would only push him away. She bit her lip and waited.

"I'll take a rain check," he replied. The mattress dipped as he sat down to put on his shoes. The bedding looked like a war zone.

At first Megan's heart soared at the promise behind the words, and then she realized he hadn't even looked at her. He was a man on the run, and it was Megan he ran from. Quietly, painfully, her heart broke in two.

She picked up Tyler, who was starting to fuss, and held him to her chest like a shield as she buried her face in his neck and inhaled his sweet baby scent. Mac fled down the stairs and she followed more slowly. At the bottom, he finally turned, panic in his eyes.

"I can't help it. I have to go." He frowned, hands jammed deep into his pockets. "Megan, I'm sorry," he began, but then he fell silent.

Pride stiffened her backbone. Her chin went up. There would be plenty of time to cry after he left. "No problem." Her smile was nearly as brittle as the pieces of her heart.

He opened his mouth, shut it, gave Tyler one silent glance filled with indecision and fled out the door, pulling it shut behind him. To Megan's ears, the quiet click echoed like a gunshot.

Mac didn't take an easy breath until he turned into the driveway to his house and heard Rusty barking. Pulling up to the garage, he shut off the motor and rested his forehead to the wheel. What the hell had he done?

When he finally went inside, the message light on his machine was blinking. Once he'd run into Megan he'd forgotten all about going back to the office as he had promised Elaine he would do. He glanced at his watch. She'd have gone home by now and he didn't want to bother her there. By tomorrow he'd come up with a plausible explanation for his lapse.

After he'd fed Rusty, Mac sat on his deck until after dark, a drink in his hand and a head full of thoughts spinning like pinwheels.

Where had everything gone so wrong? When had Megan become so important that walking away was like cutting off his own hand? And how could Tyler still mean so much to him? The kid wasn't even his.

Mac wanted to throw the empty glass as far as he could, but then he'd be out there with a flashlight picking up pieces so Rusty didn't cut his paws. He settled for slamming the heavy tumbler down on the railing so hard that the ice cubes flew out.

The phone rang from inside the house. He considered ignoring it, but changed his mind. It might be Elaine and he didn't want to worry her. When he answered, hearing his mother's voice, he wished he'd gone with his first impulse.

"We're having a dinner party this weekend," she said without preamble. "I'd like you to be there."

Mac's protective instincts went on red alert, but it took him a few moments to ferret out the reason for the summons.

"Edwin Dorchester is coming and he's bringing his daughter, Alyssa," his mother finally admitted in the face of Mac's persistence. "You know he'd take you back at the firm in a moment if you asked." Mac had worked for Dorchester before he left Denver. "And Alyssa's a widow now."

"That doesn't surprise me," Mac replied, "considering her husband's age when she married him. You wouldn't be matchmaking, would you, Mother?" Alyssa had left Mac once for a richer prospect. He had no intentions of letting that happen again.

"Of course not," she sputtered, all offended innocence. "Although you could do worse than Alyssa." She didn't add that he already had, but she was probably thinking as much.

"I doubt that."

"You're not getting any younger, and your father and I would still like a grandchild before it's too late," she persisted.

"Trust me, when it happens, it won't be with Alyssa."

His mother remained silent, waiting him out. "I don't know about this weekend," he stalled. "I'll have to call you back."

"Don't disappoint me," she warned. Without bothering to ask how he was, she said her goodbyes, reminded him again to get back to her, and rang off.

Mac wandered back outside, annoyed that he hadn't refused the invitation on the spot. He had no interest in breaking bread with Edwin Dorchester or his gold-digging daughter.

His mother's words rang in his ear. *Don't disappoint me.* How many times had he heard that over the years?

He pictured his parents, calm, practical, polite to each other, giving the appearance of quiet contentment. Appearance was all. If you stayed inside the lines, you would be rewarded. If you strayed, you had no one but yourself to blame.

Mac was obliged to carry on the family name, to provide an heir. He realized now the reason behind his own existence. His family had been bound by blood, not love, and he had very nearly carried on the tradition. He'd proposed to Megan for all the wrong reasons. He'd been fooling himself, but he hadn't fooled her. She'd seen what was missing in him.

He knew now that she and her baby were the family he was meant to have. When he'd opened his eyes earlier to find them in bed with him, he had wanted nothing more than to reach out and gather them close, but he'd been too damn scared. Bound by rules that no longer made sense.

Instead of taking a chance on his heart, he'd panicked and run. All his life he'd been good at disappointing the people he loved and perhaps he'd disappoint Megan, too. The big question now was would she give him another chance to show them both that he wouldn't?

"Hi, Mac. How have you been?" Claire Davis asked as she plopped down on the stool next to his.

Mac was sitting at the counter of the diner nursing a cup of coffee. In the last week he'd sent Megan flowers and balloons, even a whole case of peanut butter M&M's, but she still wouldn't accept his phone calls. All he got was her damn machine. He was walking a road he'd been down before. He hadn't liked it then and he didn't much care for it now.

His parents were angry that he'd missed his mother's precious dinner party and he'd lost a lucrative order at work because he'd been reluctant to leave town. Just this morning Archer had threatened to quit if Mac didn't "pull his head out of his armpit and start acting like a man and not a badger with a hangover." Even Elaine had stopped bringing coffee into his office.

"I'm fine," he replied to Dr. Davis's greeting. "Can I buy you a cup of joe?" Now why had he said that when the last thing he wanted was company?

"Sure, thanks." She set her purse on the counter. "Have you seen Tyler?" she asked as soon as Millie had filled her empty cup and departed.

He shook his head. "Not for lack of trying." Damn, what was wrong with him this morning?

Next he'd be spilling his problems like a beached tanker leaking oil.

"Oh?"

He shook his head, trying to backpedal. "It's nothing. How are you?"

Her blue eyes were sympathetic. Claire Davis was a pretty woman, unattached as far as he knew. So why didn't the male in him respond to her?

"I saw Megan the other day." She was watching him closely over the rim of her coffee cup. "Did you know she's thinking about moving?"

"To a bigger place?" he asked, doing his best to infuse his voice with idle curiosity.

"To a bigger town. Reno. I think she has a cousin there."

Mac's bad mood plummeted another notch and he forgot all about idle curiosity. "When?" he demanded.

Claire shrugged. "I'm not sure. It's not like she'd have to find a new job, so I guess she could go anytime. Of course she'd probably want to sell the townhouse first." She searched his face. "You two seemed to have something going until we broke the news about Tyler. I feel partially responsible. Are you going to let them move out of your life?"

Mac hunched over his cooling coffee, wondering how much Claire knew. "She refuses to have anything to do with me."

"You don't come across as a man who gives up easily." The doctor stirred sugar into her coffee and took another sip.

Reluctantly, Mac owned up to the flowers and candy. "Got any ideas?" he asked after Millie refilled his cup.

Claire propped her chin on her hand. "Wow, I wish someone would send me flowers."

"Anyone in particular?" Mac asked, her wistful tone making him curious.

Her cheeks went pink. "Maybe. But I have to say that unrequited attraction is a pitiful thing."

"Not unless you know it's not returned. Maybe the man in question doesn't know you're interested." He fiddled with his cup. "Anyone I know? Perhaps I can put in a word," he suggested clumsily.

"No, thanks. It's not a big deal." Two people came in and the bell over the door jingled cheerfully. "If you're serious about Megan," Claire continued, "perhaps you need to convince her."

"How am I supposed to do that when she won't take my calls?" he asked, exasperated.

She thought for a moment, lips pursed. "If you can't tell her, you'll just have to think of a way to show her. Give her a reason to stay in Buttonwood, one she can't ignore."

Before Mac could ask what kind of a gesture she had in mind, she excused herself and unclipped a cell phone from her belt. "Medical emergency," she told him after a brief conversation. "A toddler with a crayon up her nose." She squeezed his arm as she grabbed her purse and slid off the stool.

''Thanks for the coffee and good luck with your project.''

Mac hadn't tried to get Megan's attention for nearly two weeks now, she reminded herself as she walked in the door with Tyler and glared at the steady red eye on her machine. She'd been right to ignore him. He'd given up much too easily.

''It's better this way. Less painful than getting hurt later,'' she explained to Tyler as she set down his carrier so she could unload the groceries from her car.

''Mac!''

He was standing in the open doorway, a brown bag in each arm. Had he overheard?

''Hi, Megan. I hope I'm not intruding.''

Her chin went up along with her protective armor. ''Actually, you are.''

He winced as though she'd struck him, but the last thing she wanted was to test her resolve against his presence. What she and Tyler needed, she reminded herself, was commitment, not for her to have another roll in the hay with a man who could walk away at any time.

She could not, would not, subject her child to that kind of abandonment. It was too painful.

He shifted the grocery bags. ''Can I come in?''

''Only long enough to set them down,'' she warned, knowing she was losing valuable ground by letting him cross the threshold.

He went into the kitchen and put the bags on the counter. "I'd like to talk."

Like the shields of the Enterprise, Megan's defenses were firmly in place. "No, that's not a good idea."

He leaned his hip against the counter and folded his arms across his chest. "What are you afraid of?" he challenged.

"Nice try. You're not going to trick me into proving something, though. Feel free to think whatever you like." Damn, did he have to be so attractive, so utterly male that it was all she could do not to touch him? She had to get him out of here fast or she'd sink to the floor at his feet in a quivering puddle of adoration. She thought of Tyler and stiffened her resolve. "Please go."

Mac straightened and let his arms drop to his sides. "You want me out of your life? Fine, but first, come out to my house. There's something I want to show you. After that, if you still want me to leave you alone, I will."

Shaking her head, she picked up her baby and shushed him. She didn't need another visit to Mac's home. Preserving the past by restoring a lovely old house didn't necessarily mean a man was capable of realizing the importance of continuity, of commitment, of putting down the kind of roots she needed. "I don't see the point."

He took a step toward her and stopped. "Humor me," he wheedled. "If for no other reason than because I was there for you when you needed me."

Resentment washed through her at his shameless manipulation, but she couldn't deny him, and he knew it. "I'm taking my own car," she snapped.

"I'll see you there." Without a backward glance, he left her grumbling under her breath as she set Tyler in his swing, cranked up the handle and began unloading her groceries.

It was nearly an hour later that Megan pulled up next to Mac's truck in his spacious front yard. She'd stalled as long as she could, and now Tyler dozed in his car seat. The dog's barking jerked him awake and he began to cry, so she lifted him out and headed for the porch. Before she could get there, Mac opened the dark-blue front door. Rusty sat impatiently beside him, tail thumping.

"I was beginning to think you'd changed your mind," Mac said, opening the door wider.

She didn't bother to hide her annoyance as she patted Rusty's silky head. "How could I, after what you said?"

He shrugged. "All's fair in love and war."

The words made her heart stutter. What was he trying to tell her? She stared, but his expression revealed nothing.

"May I?" He held out his hands for Tyler, who was starting to squirm. Mac cuddled him expertly, talking softly while Tyler looked up at him with an expression of wonder.

Tears of regret filled Megan's eyes and she blinked them quickly away. She couldn't allow herself to be fooled into thinking Mac's attitude had changed. He might make her happy for a while, might insinuate himself into Tyler's tiny heart, but the devastation he left behind would last a lifetime.

"I heard you might be moving," he said.

"Moving?" she echoed foolishly as she trailed him inside. "Where?"

"Reno," he said over his shoulder. "Claire Davis told me."

"I can't imagine where she got a notion like that." Suspicion raised its ugly head. "What else did Claire tell you?" she asked.

Mac glanced down at his feet. "Nothing important. You aren't going anywhere?"

"I hadn't planned on it," Megan replied. "She must have been thinking of someone at the clinic."

He shrugged. "I suppose so."

"What did you want to show me?" Megan was getting impatient. Being near him was just too upsetting.

"It's out back." Holding Tyler, he led the way through the house to the deck.

When Megan saw the playhouse, a perfect miniature of Mac's house, she was filled with bittersweet yearning. Perhaps one day she would be able to afford something similar for Tyler. "It's fantastic," she murmured, descending the stairs for a closer look.

Mac and Rusty followed her as she circled the small structure. It was an identical copy, right down to the pitch of the roof, the window boxes and the gingerbread trim. Even the dark-blue front door matched. Any child would be lucky to have such a fabulous toy.

"Did you make it to use as a display model?" she asked curiously. It was obvious that a tremendous amount of work had gone into the tiny building.

"I built it for Tyler." His voice was gruff.

"But he won't be old enough to use it for years!" Megan exclaimed. Did Mac expect her to bring him over here to play? She was totally confused.

Mac led the way back up the steps and laid Tyler carefully down on a cushioned chaise. "The playhouse has one requirement," he said outrageously. "It can only belong to a child whose parents live in the house it's modeled after. Both parents."

Megan began to tremble as the meaning behind his words sank in. "What are you saying?"

"I'm telling you that the playhouse—and the daddy—will still be here for Tyler when he's old enough. The real question is, will his mother be here, too?"

Tears streamed down Megan's face, but she was barely aware of them. Damn, but Mac was making it difficult to turn him down. "I—I," she stuttered helplessly.

He held up his hand. "Wait, don't say anything. The last time I proposed, I gave you a bunch of solid, practical reasons why getting married would be a good idea."

Her heart sank. Was he about to recite that list again? To her surprise, he dropped to one knee on the deck at her feet.

"I won't bore you with a list of reasons why you and I belong together, when there are only two that matter." His dark eyes locked on hers as he reached for her hand. "I love you. I love our son. I'll be here for you both as long as I live. Will you marry me and make us the family I need so badly to make my life complete? Will you?"

Megan couldn't speak past the lump in her throat and she could barely see through her tears of joy. All she could do was to launch herself into his arms, confident that he would be there to catch her. Just as he always would.

"Yes," she finally managed to sob. "Oh, Mac, I love you, too."

With a groan of relief, he wrapped his arms around her. As he got to his feet and swung her off the ground, Rusty began to bark and Tyler let out a shriek that just had to be his personal stamp of approval.

* * * * *

*Turn the page for a sneak preview of
Diana Whitney's compelling story,*

WHO'S THAT BABY?,

*the next installment of
SO MANY BABIES.*

*Dr. Claire Davis was long attracted to
attorney Johnny Winterhawk from afar.
But not in her wildest dreams did she
ever imagine the part she'd play in
the devastatingly handsome
Native American's life!*

*On sale February 2000
only from Special Edition.*

Chapter One

He loomed in the doorway, not a tall man, but a powerful one, bronze and obsidian, copper and jet, so male that every ounce of moisture evaporated from Claire's mouth and the icy night air steamed against her heated skin.

"Good evening, Mr. Davis. I'm Dr. Winterhawk." At his blank stare, her smile stuck to her cheeks as if glued. "I mean, I'm Dr. Davis. You're Mr. Winterhawk. Of course, you already know that." Was that a giggle? Claire felt dizzy. She'd giggled, actually tittered like a silly schoolgirl. "I mean, you know who you are. You certainly don't know who I am. Except that I've just told you—"

Dear Lord, please strike me mute.

"—or at least, I've just tried to tell you, but it seems as if my tongue has a mind of its own this evening—" Another giggle. This was not acceptable, not acceptable at all.

Claire snapped her mouth shut, felt her lips curve into what must have appeared to be a demented grimace. She felt like a raving lunatic, but he was so close, so very close. Close enough to smell him, to see the gleam of bewilderment in eyes so intensely dark that a woman could get lost in them. Close enough to observe sparkling drops of milky moisture on his cheek, damp blotches on his pinstriped shirt, a puff of snowy powder marring his perfectly groomed black hair.

"Thank you for coming, Doctor." His voice was firmly resolute, but a quiver of tension caught her attention. She regarded him more analytically now, mustering enough lucidity to recognize veiled panic in his eyes. "I know what an imposition this is, but under the circumstances—"

A thin wail emanated from inside the room, barely audible beyond the cacophony of television and radio noise also blaring from inside the house. The fragile cry instantly snapped Claire into physician mode. She straightened, glancing past the impressive man to the interior of a surprisingly lush home. He'd barely stepped aside to allow her access when she pushed past him, following the sound to a tiny infant nested in a blanket-padded car seat, which had been placed on a dining-room table amidst a clutter of documents and legal briefs.

With her attention completely attuned to the child, the din of music and television chatter grated on her last nerve. ''For heaven's sake, turn off the television,'' Claire muttered. ''If I had to listen to that racket for more than five seconds, I'd cry, too.''

Johnny leapt forward to silence the television. A moment later the music ceased, and blessed silence settled over the house, broken only by the pitiful sobs of the fussy infant.

Claire set her knapsack on a chair and scooped the unhappy baby into her arms. The baby stiffened normally at the movement, flailing little arms that seemed strong, well-developed, normally coordinated. ''There, there, precious, what seems to be the trouble, hmm?'' The baby sobbed, bobbed its little head against her shoulder to gaze up with eyes as dark as those of the man who watched anxiously.

''She's been crying for over an hour,'' he said. ''I found some powdered formula—'' His gaze slipped to a diaper bag that had been opened, its contents strewn about the sofa as if eviscerated in a panic. ''I tried to feed her.''

Claire smiled, wiping the remnants of the meal from the infant's feathery black hair. Crusted formula was splotched on the baby's face, and her pajamas were saturated as well. ''Looks like she's wearing most of it.'' She angled an amused glance in his direction. ''Or perhaps you are.''

She placed the infant on the blanket, undressed her carefully, looked at the staunchly distraught man hovering nearby. "Tell me again how you happened to be, er, babysitting this evening?"

He paled slightly. "It's rather a delicate matter."

"Is it?" Resting her palm on the baby's tummy, Claire used her free hand to unsnap her case and retrieve her stethoscope. "Physicians are a discreet breed. I'll take your secrets to my grave."

He sighed, pinched the bridge of his nose. When he glanced up, the confusion in his eyes touched her. "It's just that this is...quite personal."

"So I've gathered. Since you've requested my assistance, and since the well-being of an infant is at stake, I'm obliged to ask certain questions, and frankly you are quite obliged to answer them."

A redness crawled up his flushed throat. He coughed, glanced away. "My apologies, Dr. Davis. You've gone out of your way to be helpful, and I've repaid you poorly."

Her heart fluttered. He was without a doubt the most perfect man God had ever created. Claire wondered if he was aware of that.

An irked squeak brought her attention back to the infant. Claire's heart felt as if it had been squeezed. Babies were her business. She'd seen hundreds of them, all beautiful, all adorable.

But there was something special about this black-eyed, button-nosed babe, something almost mythical and chilling. It was as if this tiny infant had the power of a magus, the eyes of an old soul trapped in a newborn body. She felt a kinship to the child, an instant bonding so sudden and forceful that her own body vibrated with it.

Claire brushed her knuckles across the silky-soft baby cheek. ''What is her name?''

Johnny yanked at his collar, skewing his tie to the side. ''Lucy.''

''Lucy,'' Claire crooned. ''A beautiful name for a beautiful girl.'' At that moment, Claire fell utterly and completely in love with this precious infant. It wasn't professional. It wasn't even rational. But it was nonetheless real. And it would change the course of her life forever.

PAMELA TOTH
DIANA WHITNEY
ALLISON LEIGH
LAURIE PAIGE
bring you four heartwarming stories in the brand-new series

So Many Babies

At the Buttonwood Baby Clinic, babies and romance abound!

On sale January 2000: **THE BABY LEGACY**
by Pamela Toth

On sale February 2000: **WHO'S THAT BABY?**
by Diana Whitney

On sale March 2000: **MILLIONAIRE'S INSTANT BABY**
by Allison Leigh

On sale April 2000: **MAKE WAY FOR BABIES!**
by Laurie Paige

Only from Silhouette SPECIAL EDITION
Available at your favorite retail outlet.

Silhouette®
Where love comes alive™

If you enjoyed what you just read,
then we've got an offer you can't resist!

Take 2 bestselling
love stories FREE!
Plus get a FREE surprise gift!

Clip this page and mail it to Silhouette Reader Service™

IN U.S.A.	IN CANADA
3010 Walden Ave.	P.O. Box 609
P.O. Box 1867	Fort Erie, Ontario
Buffalo, N.Y. 14240-1867	L2A 5X3

YES! Please send me 2 free Silhouette Special Edition® novels and my free surprise gift. Then send me 6 brand-new novels every month, which I will receive months before they're available in stores. In the U.S.A., bill me at the bargain price of $3.57 plus 25¢ delivery per book and applicable sales tax, if any*. In Canada, bill me at the bargain price of $3.96 plus 25¢ delivery per book and applicable taxes**. That's the complete price and a savings of over 10% off the cover prices—what a great deal! I understand that accepting the 2 free books and gift places me under no obligation ever to buy any books. I can always return a shipment and cancel at any time. Even if I never buy another book from Silhouette, the 2 free books and gift are mine to keep forever. So why not take us up on our invitation. You'll be glad you did!

235 SEN CNFD
335 SEN CNFE

Name	(PLEASE PRINT)	
Address	Apt.#	
City	State/Prov.	Zip/Postal Code

* Terms and prices subject to change without notice. Sales tax applicable in N.Y.
** Canadian residents will be charged applicable provincial taxes and GST.
   All orders subject to approval. Offer limited to one per household.
   ® are registered trademarks of Harlequin Enterprises Limited.

SPED99   ©1998 Harlequin Enterprises Limited

SILHOUETTE'S 20TH ANNIVERSARY CONTEST
OFFICIAL RULES
NO PURCHASE NECESSARY TO ENTER

1. To enter, follow directions published in the offer to which you are responding. Contest begins 1/1/00 and ends on 8/24/00 (the "Promotion Period"). Method of entry may vary. Mailed entries must be postmarked by 8/24/00, and received by 8/31/00.

2. During the Promotion Period, the Contest may be presented via the Internet. Entry via the Internet may be restricted to residents of certain geographic areas that are disclosed on the Web site. To enter via the Internet, if you are a resident of a geographic area in which Internet entry is permissible, follow the directions displayed on-line, including typing your essay of 100 words or fewer telling us "Where In The World Your Love Will Come Alive." On-line entries must be received by 11:59 p.m. Eastern Standard time on 8/24/00. Limit one e-mail entry per person, household and e-mail address per day, per presentation. If you are a resident of a geographic area in which entry via the Internet is permissible, you may, in lieu of submitting an entry on-line, enter by mail, by hand-printing your name, address, telephone number and contest number/name on an 8"x 11" plain piece of paper and telling us in 100 words or fewer "Where In The World Your Love Will Come Alive," and mailing via first-class mail to: Silhouette 20th Anniversary Contest, (in the U.S.) P.O. Box 9069, Buffalo, NY 14269-9069; (In Canada) P.O. Box 637, Fort Erie, Ontario, Canada L2A 5X3. Limit one 8"x 11" mailed entry per person, household and e-mail address per day. On-line and/or 8"x 11" mailed entries received from persons residing in geographic areas in which Internet entry is not permissible will be disqualified. No liability is assumed for lost, late, incomplete, inaccurate, nondelivered or misdirected mail, or misdirected e-mail, for technical, hardware or software failures of any kind, lost or unavailable network connection, or failed, incomplete, garbled or delayed computer transmission or any human error which may occur in the receipt or processing of the entries in the contest.

3. Essays will be judged by a panel of members of the Silhouette editorial and marketing staff based on the following criteria:

    Sincerity (believability, credibility)—50%
    Originality (freshness, creativity)—30%
    Aptness (appropriateness to contest ideas)—20%

    Purchase or acceptance of a product offer does not improve your chances of winning. In the event of a tie, duplicate prizes will be awarded.

4. All entries become the property of Harlequin Enterprises Ltd., and will not be returned. Winner will be determined no later than 10/31/00 and will be notified by mail. Grand Prize winner will be required to sign and return Affidavit of Eligibility within 15 days of receipt of notification. Noncompliance within the time period may result in disqualification and an alternative winner may be selected. All municipal, provincial, federal, state and local laws and regulations apply. Contest open only to residents of the U.S. and Canada who are 18 years of age or older, and is void wherever prohibited by law. Internet entry is restricted solely to residents of those geographical areas in which Internet entry is permissible. Employees of Torstar Corp., their affiliates, agents and members of their immediate families are not eligible. Taxes on the prizes are the sole responsibility of winners. Entry and acceptance of any prize offered constitutes permission to use winner's name, photograph or other likeness for the purposes of advertising, trade and promotion on behalf of Torstar Corp. without further compensation to the winner, unless prohibited by law. Torstar Corp and D.L. Blair, Inc., their parents, affiliates and subsidiaries, are not responsible for errors in printing or electronic presentation of contest or entries. In the event of printing or other errors which may result in unintended prize values or duplication of prizes, all affected contest materials or entries shall be null and void. If for any reason the Internet portion of the contest is not capable of running as planned, including infection by computer virus, bugs, tampering, unauthorized intervention, fraud, technical failures, or any other causes beyond the control of Torstar Corp. which corrupt or affect the administration, secrecy, fairness, integrity or proper conduct of the contest, Torstar Corp. reserves the right, at its sole discretion, to disqualify any individual who tampers with the entry process and to cancel, terminate, modify or suspend the contest or the Internet portion thereof. In the event of a dispute regarding an on-line entry, the entry will be deemed submitted by the authorized holder of the e-mail account submitted at the time of entry. Authorized account holder is defined as the natural person who is assigned to an e-mail address by an Internet access provider, on-line service provider or other organization that is responsible for arranging e-mail address for the domain associated with the submitted e-mail address.

5. Prizes: Grand Prize—a $10,000 vacation to anywhere in the world. Travelers (at least one must be 18 years of age or older) or parent or guardian if one traveler is a minor, must sign and return a Release of Liability prior to departure. Travel must be completed by December 31, 2001, and is subject to space and accommodations availability. Two hundred (200) Second Prizes—a two-book limited edition autographed collector set from one of the Silhouette Anniversary authors: Nora Roberts, Diana Palmer, Linda Howard or Annette Broadrick (value $10.00 each set). All prizes are valued in U.S. dollars.

6. For a list of winners (available after 10/31/00), send a self-addressed, stamped envelope to: Harlequin Silhouette 20th Anniversary Winners, P.O. Box 4200, Blair, NE 68009-4200.

Contest sponsored by Torstar Corp., P.O. Box 9042, Buffalo, NY 14269-9042.

ENTER FOR
A CHANCE TO WIN*

Silhouette's 20th Anniversary Contest

Tell Us Where in the World
You Would Like *Your* Love To Come Alive...
And We'll Send the Lucky Winner There!

Silhouette wants to take you wherever
your happy ending can come true.

Here's how to enter: Tell us, in 100 words or less,
where you want to go to make your love come alive!

In addition to the grand prize, there will be 200
runner-up prizes, collector's-edition book sets
autographed by one of the Silhouette anniversary
authors: **Nora Roberts, Diana Palmer,
Linda Howard** or **Annette Broadrick**.

DON'T MISS YOUR CHANCE TO WIN!
ENTER NOW! No Purchase Necessary

Name: _____

Address: _____

City: _____ State/Province: _____

Zip/Postal Code: _____

Mail to Harlequin Books: **In the U.S.**: P.O. Box 9069, Buffalo, NY
14269-9069; **In Canada**: P.O. Box 637, Fort Erie, Ontario, L4A 5X3

COMING NEXT MONTH

#1303 MAN...MERCENARY...MONARCH—Joan Elliott Pickart
Royally Wed
In the blink of an eye, John Colton discovered he was a Crown Prince, a brand-new father...and a man on the verge of falling for a woman in *his* royal family's employ. Yet trust—and love—didn't come easily to this one-time mercenary who desperately wanted to be son, brother, father...*husband?*

#1304 DR. MOM AND THE MILLIONAIRE—Christine Flynn
Prescription: Marriage
No woman had been able to get the powerful Chase Harrington anywhere near an altar. Then again, this confirmed bachelor had never met someone like the charmingly fascinating Dr. Alexandra Larson, a woman whose tender loving care promised to heal him, body, heart...and soul.

#1305 WHO'S THAT BABY?—Diana Whitney
So Many Babies
Johnny Winterhawk did what any red-blooded male would when he found a baby on his doorstep—he panicked. Pediatrician Claire Davis rescued him by offering her hand in a marriage of convenience...and then showed him just how real a family they could be.

#1306 CATTLEMAN'S COURTSHIP—Lois Faye Dyer
Experience made Quinn Bowdrie a tough man of the land who didn't need anybody. That is, until he met the sweetly tempting Victoria Denning, the only woman who could teach this stubborn rancher the pleasures of courtship.

#1307 THE MARRIAGE BASKET—Sharon De Vita
The Blackwell Brothers
Rina Roberts had her heart set on adopting her orphaned nephew. But the boy's godfather, Hunter Blackwell, stood in her way. Their love for the child drew them together and Rina knew that not only did the handsome doctor hold the key to Billy's future—but also to her own heart.

#1308 FALLING FOR AN OLDER MAN—Trisha Alexander
Callahans & Kin
Sheila Callahan dreamed of picket fences and wedding rings, but Jack Kinsella, the man of her dreams, wasn't the slightest bit interested in commitment, especially not to his best friend's younger sister. But one night together created more than just passion....